KINSELLA'S REVENGE

Newton, Kansas, was a cow town in 1871, when bounty hunter twin brothers Fin and Ray Kinsella became involved in what was to be called 'the Newton General Massacre'. It was to lead Ray on the road to revenge. Along the way, Ray and the three-man posse met up with Kitty Brown, sole survivor of a family murdered by one of the men they were tracking. She joined the posse on a ride that would change all their lives. And, when the shooting stopped, revenge from beyond the grave would come to haunt them all.

Books by Mark Falcon
in the Linford Western Library:

THE OUTLAW'S WOMAN

MARK FALCON

KINSELLA'S REVENGE

Complete and Unabridged

LINFORD
Leicester

First published in Great Britain in 2004 by
Robert Hale Limited
London

First Linford Edition
published 2005
by arrangement with
Robert Hale Limited
London

British Library CIP Data

Falcon, Mark
    Kinsella's revenge.—Large print ed.—
Linford western library
1. Western stories
2. Large type books
I. Title
823.9'14 [F]

ISBN 1–84395–915–1

Published by
F. A. Thorpe (Publishing)
Anstey, Leicestershire

Set by Words & Graphics Ltd.
Anstey, Leicestershire
Printed and bound in Great Britain by
T. J. International Ltd., Padstow, Cornwall

This book is printed on acid-free paper

to 'the twins, Philip & Ronald'
and
John and Keith

1

The two men dismounted in what seemed like one single movement. It was usual for this to happen as the Kinsella brothers were twins. They were so close that they could often read each other's thoughts and no words were necessary. It came in useful in their line of work for they were bounty hunters.

Finlay Kinsella was the elder by twenty minutes and was the more dominant of the two, but Ray had always accepted this; he tended to look up to his elder sibling and usually allowed Fin to lead.

Ray touched his twin's arm and pointed ahead without uttering a word. Fin nodded. He had seen their quarry whom they had been trailing for a month now from Missouri into Kansas. The man, Ned Bodine, had pitched camp for the night at the foot of a cliff.

He was obviously unaware of the Kinsellas' close proximity. He had not been the only one who had been lulled into a false sense of security for the brothers were highly trained trackers. They had been well taught by a half-breed Sioux they had fought alongside in the Civil War. Johnny Diamond had also shown them how to draw and fire a weapon with deadly precision. Now, the Kinsellas were even more proficient than their tutor. Both brothers were confident of the outcome each time they were drawn into a gunfight.

Fin pointed to himself, then indicated that he would go around to the right and for Ray to go to the left of the outlaw wanted for murder.

Ray waited a while as his brother got into position before he moved away to the left. They were both as silent as shadows and Bodine was occupied lighting a fire for his coffee pot.

They could easily have just shot the man but it was not their way. They

2

employed their usual method and Ray moved up behind him.

Bodine felt his flesh crawl along his back at the pressure of the Colt revolver's barrel.

'Easy now, Bodine,' Ray soothed as he transferred his gun into his left hand and eased the outlaw's gun out of its holster.

'I suggest you put your hands up high,' he said equally quietly, like the hiss of a snake.

When the man's hands rose in the air, Fin came forward, a slight smile on his good-looking face.

The flames had taken on the kindling and there was just enough light for the outlaw to see the two men holding guns on him. He blinked several times, his mouth opening wide.

'Am I seein' things?' he gasped. 'You're both the same!'

'That's right, mister. You're not hallucinating,' Fin told him. He took out a Wanted poster from the pocket of his shirt and unfolded the squares. He compared the likeness with the real thing and nodded to his brother.

'Yeah, he's the one we've been after, Ray.'

'He's wanted dead or alive, Fin.' Ray turned to Bodine. 'Which is it to be, fella?' he asked. 'Are you coming quietly, or would you rather have a shoot-out with either of us?'

Bodine grunted. 'You mean you'd give me back my gun?' he asked incredulously.

'Sure.' Fin smiled.

'Huh! There are two of you. If I draw on you, the other'll shoot me, so what chance do I have?'

'A fifty-fifty chance,' Ray told him. 'Pick which one you want to go against and the other will stay out of it.'

Bodine weighed it up before answering.

'What if I kill one of you? What's to stop the other killing me afterwards?'

'You've got our word that we won't — unless of course you try and take the other one of us on afterwards.'

4

The three faced each other for a few moments before Fin spoke.

'Well, Bodine, what's it gonna be?'

'How do *I* know which one of you to go against?'

Ray produced a dollar coin from his Levis' pocket.

'Heads it's Fin, Tails it's me.'

Bodine still did not like the idea, but it was the only chance he was likely to get.

'I always pick heads,' he said, 'so heads it'll be.'

Ray tossed the coin and held the palm of his right hand over the coin in his left hand. He left it there for a few seconds to heighten the tension then, with a smile, uncovered the coin.

'It's your lucky day, Mr Bodine. It's tails.'

Ned Bodine did not feel at all lucky. Which one of these two identical men was the faster? he wondered. Both were very confident and that very fact unnerved him. His whole life seemed to flash before him and a mean, unworthy life it had been too. He knew he deserved to die for all the bad things he had done but he came to the conclusion that dying from a bullet would be far better than hanging from a gallows.

'OK, let's get on with it. Let me check my gun first though.'

Ray handed the man back his gun, at the same time holding his own on him while he checked the weapon and put it back into its holster. Ray replaced his own and stood back a few paces.

'When you're ready, Bodine,' Ray told him.

Bodine's heart was beating rapidly. It made his hands shake, which was not what he wanted right now.

'Get on with it!' Fin broke in.

Fin's words made up Bodine's mind and he drew his weapon at the same time as Ray did his own. But only one shot was fired which seemed to echo and reverberate in the rocks behind them.

The outlaw Ned Bodine fell in a

crumpled heap, a bullet in his evil heart.

Fin bent to examine the body and nodded in satisfaction that the man was really dead.

'It's a shame the coffee pot wasn't put on to boil before this all started,' Ray remarked calmly. 'We could have been drinking coffee by now.'

'Yeah,' Fin nodded a little sadly. 'We'll have to plan these things a little better next time.'

Ray's white teeth flashed in a smile in the flickering firelight.

The two bounty hunters prepared supper, which consisted of a jack-rabbit Fin had shot earlier. They were short of supplies but would stock up again at the nearest town that had some kind of law in it. They guessed it would be Newton, now a cowtown. It was only a month or two old and the first place the rails had reached so far. News had spread fast and herds of cattle mostly from Texas were arriving each week to be transported East.

★ ★ ★

Two days after the demise of Ned
Bodine, the two bounty hunters were
riding into Newton, Bodine's body tied
over his horse. Those on the sidewalks
stopped in their tracks, their mouths
open. Never in their lives before had
any of them seen two identical men.

Fin and Ray were used to the startled
looks and ignored them. They had been
subjected to a lot of abuse one way or
another from various people, too
ignorant to accept that it was possible
for two babies to be born almost at
once, who had grown into men. They
had paid dearly at school and were
often set upon by the bullies who can
always be found in school and life in
general. They had been forced to stand
back to back and fend them off, and in
the end it was the bullies who had paid
dearly. In the end, the twins were left
alone, so much alone in fact that the
two boys were friends with no one else
but each other. That was the way they

liked it. To them, everyone else was an inferior being.

The two dismounted outside the office of the town marshal and the board outside proclaimed him to be TOM CARSON.

The man inside looked up at the two as they entered. He gave them another look and blinked.

'Two for the price of one, eh?' he grinned. 'What can I do for you gents?'

Fin answered first. 'We've got a dead wanted man outside on his horse by the name of Ned Bodine. The poster says there's a five hundred dollar reward for him.'

Carson got up from behind his desk and followed the brothers outside. He took hold of the dead outlaw's hair and pulled his head up to have a look at his face. Ray showed him the poster so he could compare it.

'Looks like him. Follow me and I'll pay you. Then you can leave the body with the undertaker.'

Fin nodded and the two went back

inside the office for their bounty money.

'Have you got any more you want bringing in?' asked Fin.

'I dare say. There's no end to the paperwork I get to deal with. As if I've nothing better to do,' the lawman grumbled. He hadn't been town marshal for long, but he was already becoming tired of it. There had been more violence in the last few months than in most of the other towns Carson had been in.

After delivering Bodine's body to the undertaker the two hunters decided to get cleaned up and find a bed for the night. But night had not yet come and on the other side of the track no one seemed to sleep. It would be a night they would never forget and one which would go down in history to be known as 'the Newton General Massacre'.

2

Ray and Fin took a double room at a boarding-house on the respectable side of the street. It seemed clean but sparsely furnished, but as they only intended to use it for one night it hardly mattered.

They both washed, donned a clean set of clothes each and combed their dark-brown hair down flat with water. They also shaved, leaving their long moustaches which they twisted at the ends.

After inspecting their reflections in the mirror over the wash-stand, they were satisfied that their Aunt Martha would have been proud of their appearance. She had brought them up from new-born babies after their mother had died in childbirth. Their father, Bill, had left them with her, and the twins and his sister Martha had not set eyes on him since that day.

The boys were well cared for in spite of little money, Bill Kinsella sending what he could each month for their keep. They had a strict, puritanical upbringing but had never received any real love from the tall, thin woman who never smiled. On thinking it over, the boys realized she had little to smile about and understood just how hard it must have been for Martha Kinsella trying to make ends meet.

Ray and Fin had been forced to learn the scriptures by heart and woe betide them if they did not concentrate on the task in hand. They were made to scrub their hands until they were raw. 'Cleanliness is next to Godliness' was Martha's well-used motto. It had made the boys detest any dirt, on their hands and on their clothes. Their fastidiousness had almost become an obsession.

At the age of fourteen Martha had found them employment, Fin with the local newspaper proprietor who taught him how to set the typeface and use the press. The only objection Fin found with the work was that the ink made his hands black and was difficult to remove.

Ray was apprenticed to the local undertaker and taught how to make coffins. He had enjoyed making the dearer ones as they looked much better than the crude 'packing-case' type the poor were forced to buy for their deceased loved-ones. These were also used for dead criminals as the county had to pay for them.

After their fourteenth birthday the money from their father for their keep ceased. No one knew if Bill Kinsella was still alive or dead and if alive, where he could be contacted.

The brothers had stayed with their aunt, taking care of her now she had grown old, but she had died just before the war when they were eighteen. They had enlisted on the Confederate side as they were Missourians, but most of the skirmishes were with the neighbouring state of Kansas, which was on the Unionist side.

Although the year was now 1871, there was still much hostility between Northerners and Southerners, especially in Kansas, and more especially now that the cow herds were driven up from the Texas South to the new Newton railhead.

The Texans were a rowdy, unruly breed. A single Texas Ranger could control them with no difficulty, but the cowboys, through deep resentment and hatred for the ex-Unionists, refused to observe any of the laws made for a peaceful coexistence of the two factions who should now be one. The Texans especially, refused to let an abolitionist arrest them. Many of the ex-Confederates still wore their Rebel grey uniforms as a form of defiance.

★   ★   ★

Both brothers checked their guns and stowed them away in the holsters. They left their room and clomped down the stairs, along a short dark corridor and out into the street. Where their boarding-house was situated it was relatively quiet, but in the direction they were heading bawdy laughter, blasphemous language and the occasional gunshot could be heard. It would have been far safer if they had stayed in their room, but they were not afraid of trouble. Those days were long gone.

They were entering the red-light district of Hyde Park. Men, mostly cowboys, were entering or leaving the various houses of ill-repute after visiting the soiled doves inside. Some of these places were well run, but on the outskirts of town were many 'cribs' which housed a solitary prostitute in each and were less sanitary.

Ray and Fin visited neither. Their main interest was the gaming-tables. They were both as good at playing poker as they were bounty hunters.

The date was Friday 11 August 1871. Ray and Fin entered one of the saloons, allowing the batwing doors to swing shut behind them. As was usual, they found all eyes were upon them. They surveyed the smoke-filled room and noticed that the poker table was in the far corner. They made their way there, ignoring the stares as they pushed their way through the crowd.

'Any chance of a game?' Fin asked the four men at the table.

'Have you got a stake?' enquired the eldest of the four, a man in his early fifties, sturdily built with greying brown hair and a moustache to match.

'Sure,' Fin answered.

'We'll finish this hand, then you can join in,' said the same man.

Fin and Ray each pulled up a chair and sat down. They quietly watched the four already at the table play their game. One of the men, obviously a Texan, was referred to as Bill. A while later, they found out that the eldest of the four was also called Bill, but one of the men also called him 'Kinsella'. Ray and Fin's ears pricked up at this and they exchanged glances. Kinsella was not a common name and their own father's name was William — or Bill.

As they continued to watch and listen, they noticed a night policeman enter the room and order a whiskey. His eyes immediately went over to the table where the brothers were sitting. They guessed he was looking at them as they were used to this by now after twenty-seven years. But they were wrong on this occasion. The object of the lawman's stare was the Texan, Bill Bailey, alias William Wilson.

The night policeman downed his whiskey in one gulp and ordered another. From the look of him, Ray and Fin guessed he had already consumed a fair amount of liquor in other saloons.

Bill Kinsella glanced over at the two brothers on numerous occasions. The two could see the deepening frown on the man's brow and guessed he was thinking about them. Could these young men, obviously twins, possibly be . . . his sons?

The game finished and the man

called Bill Kinsella raked in his winnings. It was not often he left the table poorer than he started the game.

Bill Bailey (or Wilson) downed his whiskey in disgust at losing again, pushed back his chair and walked to the bar for another before the new game commenced.

'I heard you called Bill Kinsella,' said Fin. 'Did you by any chance have twin sons?'

Kinsella senior's mouth opened and seemed to stay open for a few moments.

'What are your names, boys?' he asked them, looking from one to the other.

'I'm Finlay and my brother here is Raymond — Fin and Ray.

'My God!' he said quietly. 'After all these years. How old are you now?'

'Twenty-seven,' Ray answered for them both. 'Why did you desert us like that, Pa? Why didn't you come and see us once in a while?'

Bill Kinsella looked down at the

card-table and seemed genuinely ashamed.

'I can only ask your forgiveness, sons. I didn't think I'd be much use to you as a father. You both needed a woman to care for you after your mother died having you. Your aunt Martha was the only woman I could think of. She took good care of you, didn't she?'

'Sure,' said Ray. 'She did her best under the circumstances. We never went hungry — not often anyway.'

They carried on their conversation, catching up on the time that had passed.

Meanwhile Bill Bailey had ordered his whiskey at the bar. Bailey had consumed a fair amount of alcohol himself by this time.

'You, Bailey!' Mike McCluskie, the night policeman, was grinding his teeth in anger as he faced the Texan.

Bailey gave him a casual glance as he picked up his whiskey.

'What do you want?' Bailey asked defiantly.

'You know,' McCluskie hissed. 'Leave Clara alone. She's mine!'

'Yours?' Bailey grinned. 'She's a prostitute. She's *anybody*'s who's got the price. A nice little lay she is, too.'

'You keep away from her — you hear? I'm gonna kill you!' McCluskie exclaimed, swaying a little from intoxication.

Bill Bailey ran out of the Red Front saloon in a mighty hurry, followed by McCluskie who already had his pistol drawn. Bailey crouched in the dark but McCluskie saw him and shot him down.

A crowd gathered round the body and found Bailey was not quite dead.

Someone shouted, 'Take him to the Santa Fe hotel!'

Bailey was taken there and a doctor called, but by this time the Texan was dead.

'Seems like we've got a player missing now,' said Bill Kinsella when news of Bailey's demise came to them. It was not long, however, before another man joined the table and the new game commenced.

3

Now that Ray and Fin had met their father, they were reluctant to leave Newton until they had got to know him better. Maybe a little break would not hurt, they decided. It had been some time since they had taken a holiday.

Playing poker through the night and well into the early morning, meant the Kinsellas rose late the next morning, meeting up at around noon at the Santa Fe hotel where Bill Kinsella was booked in.

As they had missed breakfast, the lunch menu was perused and steaks ordered all round.

'Well, Pa,' Fin began as they sat at one of the tables, 'what have you been doing with yourself all these years? We've got a lot to catch up on.'

Bill Kinsella found he could not look

his new-found sons in the eye with his reply.

'I've moved around a lot,' he began. 'I got into a bit of trouble down in Texas and spent five years in jail.'

Ray frowned. 'What did you do?' he asked him.

'I had a fight with a man over a poker-game. He called me a cheat and I shot him — although he did draw first,' he added.

Ray and Fin were disappointed. They had hoped their father would have done better for himself during all these years. It appeared that he hadn't amounted to much. But he was their father, their only living relative, and who were they to feel ashamed of him?

'And did you cheat, Pa?' Fin asked.

Bill shook his head. 'I don't need to cheat, son. Even if I do say so myself, I'm a pretty good poker-player. It's not often I leave the table poorer than I started.'

Ray grinned. 'Yeah, we had noticed!'

Bill shrugged his shoulders. 'Maybe

that's why some think I cheat, 'cos I'm usually so lucky.'

'Haven't you ever done anything other than play poker?' Fin asked him.

'I ran a livery stable for a while. I even did my bit in the war. Apart from that . . . ' Bill shrugged his shoulders.

★   ★   ★

The episode in the Red Front saloon on 11 August had further repercussions. Bill Bailey, who had been killed that night, had numerous friends among the Texan cowboys. They had all come up the Chisholm Trail together with a herd. Hugh Anderson was the kind of young fellow with a big chip on his shoulder and was considered to be a bit unstable. He decided that Bill Bailey's death should be avenged. He gathered several of his friends together at around midnight on Saturday 19 August. They walked together into Perry Tuttle's dance-hall and over to the gaming-table. Mike

McCluskie, who had shot Bill Bailey, was sitting with his dealt hand. The three Kinsellas were sitting in on the game at the time.

'You're a cowardly dog!' Anderson screamed at McCluskie. 'I'm going to blow the top of your head off!' He fired twice at McCluskie, a bullet entering the night policeman's neck. In spite of this, McCluskie managed to stagger to his feet and pull the trigger of his revolver. The hammer failed to detonate the cap and McCluskie collapsed on to the floor. Anderson then shot the man in the back.

The poker game was abandoned and Bill Kinsella and his two sons moved out of the way. It was not their fight and they had no intention of being recipients of stray bullets.

A young man had been watching what had happened. He pulled his gun and began blazing away at the cowboys present. Battle then commenced and bystanders dived for cover. A chair was hurled at the lights and gun flashes could be seen in the darkness.

Ray reckoned the shooting lasted about a minute and cries of the wounded could be heard. When light returned to the room it revealed utter carnage.

Anderson, who had started it all by killing Mike McCluskie, lay in a pool of his own blood, writhing and moaning in pain. The dead bodies of three of his trail crew lay dead, named as Jim Martin, Billy Garrett and Henry Kearns. Jim Wilkerson, another hand, was badly wounded. Pat Lee, a railwayman was mortally shot through the stomach, and the young man who had caused all this mayhem was nowhere to be seen. No one knew his name.

Tom Carson (nephew of the famous Kit Carson) entered the dance-hall and stopped abruptly at the scene before him. The surviving Texans moved towards the lawman and he felt himself propelled outside. He realized that to try and arrest them would have caused a street riot and was forced to withdraw.

Bill Kinsella and his sons learned that Hugh Anderson was found guilty of the murder of Mike McCluskie by a Newton coroner's jury at eight o'clock the next morning. Somehow the wounded Hugh Anderson had been spirited away by his friends.

★   ★   ★

The next evening there were other events which affected the Kinsellas.

Back in the Red Front saloon Bill Kinsella was in the same chair where Fin and Ray had first seen him over a week ago. It was time to move on, the brothers had decided. There were more criminals out there to be brought in, dead or alive, and a week of excitement in gambling places was quite enough for them. They would be sorry to say goodbye to their father, but they knew there was not much more to be learned from him and he obviously was not going anywhere.

A game had finished and Bill Kinsella clawed in his winnings. One of the players in particular looked angry as he had been completely cleaned out. Ray needed to relieve himself and also get another drink. It all happened in those few minutes while he was away from the table.

Two shots came from inside the saloon just before Ray re-entered it. He had become used to gunfire of late and did not take too much notice, but when he glanced over at the table his father and brother had been sitting at and saw them both lying on the floor, a bullet in each of their hearts, Ray's own heart seemed to stop beating for a second or two. He stood transfixed to the spot and he felt unable to move a muscle. It was as if he, too, had been shot. Half of him no longer existed. When eventually he came to his senses he noticed that the fourth man who had been sitting in on the game was no longer there.

Ray pushed his way through the men

beginning to huddle over the bodies and felt for a pulse in both of them.

'What happened?' Ray asked brokenly.

'The fella at your table accused Bill of cheating. He shot him as he said it and then shot your brother,' one of the cowboys informed him.

'Where did the fella go who was sitting here with us?' Ray yelled.

'He lit out the back way.' Someone pointed to the side of the bar where there was a door.

There was nothing more Ray could do for his father and brother. He rushed through the door after the killer. He looked up and down the street. The man was nowhere to be seen.

A night policeman, Les Talbot, was walking towards him. He had heard the gunshot and was on his way to see what had happened.

'Someone shot my pa and brother in the Red Front. Have you seen anyone running?' Ray asked.

'A man ran across to Maisie's place. Maybe it was him. He was a tall fella wearing a blue shirt.'

'That's him. I'm gonna kill him!' Ray hissed menacingly.

'Hold on there, fella. I'll come with you. He might do more damage and we don't want those doves shot up.'

Ray knew the man was referring to the prostitutes. They entered the building which had a red light in the window. Ray had never visited one of these establishments before and had often wondered what they were like. Women in various stages of undress draped themselves on red velvet *chaises-longues* as they waited for the next customer. They looked up expectantly as the two men walked over to them.

'Evening, gents. We're here for your pleasure.' One of them smiled at Ray and the policeman.

'Sorry, Doris, but we're not here for pleasure just now,' the night policeman grinned. Ray guessed he had visited the place before on more than one occasion.

'Where did the fella go who came in here just now?' Les Talbot asked.

'Upstairs, number six. Anything wrong, Les?'

'He's just killed two men in the Red Front. He'll be dangerous when cornered, I reckon. I hope none of the ladies get hurt.'

'So do I, Les,' Doris called after them as they mounted the stairs.

There was a row of doors along the corridor at the top of the staircase. They soon found number six. Les and Ray drew their guns and Les tried the door handle. It turned and the two men rushed in.

One of the doves was in the bed and looked alarmed at the sudden entrance of the two men. The open window and billowing curtain told them that the killer of the two Kinsellas in the Red Front saloon had left that way a moment or so before they arrived.

There was a balcony all around the building and as Ray and Les stepped out on to it they saw below them a man wearing a blue shirt jumping on to a horse which was awaiting him. Three other riders, who had obviously brought the mount for him, were ready to make their escape.

'Hold it right there, all of you!' Les yelled down at the four men. They looked up at the balcony but wasted no time hanging around. The man in the blue shirt fired up at Les and Ray as a parting shot, but the bullet missed them. Ray and Les aimed at their backs, but the men were already riding towards the railtracks.

'They were sure quick off the mark, bringing the killer a mount. They must have left their horses close by. Mine's at the livery stable on the other side of the track,' said Ray. 'They'll be long gone by the time I get to it.'

'We'd best find the marshal and form a posse,' Les told him as they clattered back down the stairs. 'I'll arrange for the bodies of your pa and brother to be taken to the mortuary.'

Ray nodded. He followed the night

policeman back into the Red Front. His heart turned cold at seeing Bill and Fin still lying where they had fallen.

'Anyone know what happened?' Les asked the assembled crowd.

He was given the same story that Ray had heard when he asked this question earlier.

'Was your pa cheating?' Les asked Ray.

'I'm sure he wasn't.' Ray shook his head. 'He was just a naturally lucky player, that's all. If men can't afford to lose, then they shouldn't play.'

Les got the two dead Kinsellas moved from the Red Front and everyone continued the evening as though nothing had happened. The killings had become so frequent that another was not unusual enough to warrant feelings of regret.

4

Ray fetched his horse from the livery stable and met the marshal, Tom Carson, and three men whom Ray had never met before outside the marshal's office. Carson would remain in town, but had already deputized the three to become the posse, then quickly deputized Ray who was going with them. He felt this was wasting valuable time, but without argument he allowed the legal ceremony to proceed before he went after the man who had killed his family.

'The four men who lit outa here hadn't packed supplies, I reckon,' said Ray. 'I suggest we do. They'll have to stop somewhere along the line for food and water. We'll have the advantage of them by being prepared.'

Tom Carson gave a small smile.

'I should listen to this man, men.

He's a bounty hunter by trade and knows what he's talking about.'

The three posse members nodded in agreement and accompanied Ray who led them to the general store. It was shut, but after the four had banged loudly on the door and shouted up at the window where the proprietor lived and slept, an angry storekeeper eventually opened up.

Within half an hour the four rode out of Newton in search of the killer and his three companions who had helped him escape.

'My guess is they'll make their way back to Texas,' Ray muttered as they rode.

'What if you're wrong?' Bob Daniels asked him. 'We'll lose 'em if they head off in another direction.'

'We'll ride south anyway,' Ray said firmly. 'Our hunches are usually right.'

'*Our* hunches?' asked John Roday.

For a brief moment Ray had forgotten that he could no longer include his brother in anything. He felt a sudden pang of pain at this thought.

'My brother and me,' Ray explained quietly.

'You were twins, weren't you?' Reg Toomy asked.

'Yeah.' The word came out like a sigh, which did not go unnoticed by the three men by his side.

'Weird.' Daniels shrugged his shoulders.

Ray shot him a savage glance. He and Fin had been subjected to many unkind descriptions such as this over the years and had been in many fights over it, but when they became men they just ignored the remarks and put it down to ignorance.

It was becoming lighter and Ray took this opportunity to look for fresh tracks. He rode in a line across his three companions and moved from left to right in zigzag movements. Eventually he raised his hand and pointed in a direction he was sure the four men they were trailing had gone.

The posse looked at each other. They

had not seen anything of significance that would suggest to them in which direction to go, but Ray Kinsella obviously had. There was no option but to follow his lead as they were well aware of his previous experience of bringing felons to justice — dead or alive.

* * *

Five miles away from the posse, Bert Mayhew, the killer of Bill and Fin Kinsella and his three trail-crew bunkies were filling their canteens from a creek.

'No sign of a posse yet,' Bert remarked.

'That don't mean to say there's not one following us,' Rory Yates answered. 'We got a bit of a head start on any posse though, I reckon.'

'Did you *have* to go and kill them two in the Red Front saloon, Bert?' Tom Watts chipped in.

'That fella Bill Kinsella was cheatin',

I'll bet my boots on it!' Bert offered in defence.

'And was the other fella you shot cheating, too?' Nathan Ross added to the conversation.

'I'm not sure about him, but he was about to draw his gun as I shot Bill, so I had no choice but to kill him as well.'

Ross shrugged his shoulders. 'If you say so, Bert.'

Bert looked angry at this. 'I *do* say so! I'm cleaned out now. I've hardly got a dime to my name.'

'None of us has got much money left,' Tom Watts informed him. 'After all that time on the trail, we end up with practically nothing to show for it. It hardly seems worth the trouble.'

'Yeah.' Yates nodded. 'Newton was glad enough to take our money, but they sure as hell didn't want *us*. I've a damned good mind to go back to that town and shoot it up. That'll teach 'em to have a bit more respect for us Rebs.'

'I don't reckon that would be such a good idea, Rory.' Nathan grinned.

'We'd come out on the losin' side — yet again,' he added, referring to the Civil War.

Rory growled, but did not reply to this last statement.

They continued their flight from the town of Newton and rode until midday. It was then that Bert's horse threw a shoe. Bert rode back a way looking for it, but it was nowhere to be found.

'Hell!' Bert shouted. 'The horse'll go lame if I don't soon fix a new shoe.'

'We'd best look out for habitation. We could get it fixed there, mebbe. Or we could swap it for a fresh mount,' Rory Yates suggested.

The others nodded, but it was a couple of hours later before they came across a sod-built house — and a horse in a corral.

As the four rode up to the door of the crudely built house, a middle-aged man came to the door, a rifle in his hand.

'What do you want?' he asked suspiciously.

'I want to exchange the horse I'm

riding for the one in your corral,' Bert informed him.

'Why should I do that?' the man asked him.

' 'Cos I say so,' said Bert.

'Nothing doing, mister. Now all of you, get off my land! Now!' the homesteader ordered.

'Sorry you feel that way,' said Bert, and turned his mount's head back in the direction they had come from. The others did likewise, giving Bert a strange, enquiring look.

Bert Mayhew carefully drew his gun from its holster and turned in the saddle. The homesteader was not expecting what happened next and there was a look of surprise on his face as he fell forward, dropping his rifle by his side. A woman and a young boy had come to the doorway and Bert shot them down also, so there would be no witnesses left.

Bert's three companions looked askance at what he had just done, but any feelings of remorse were soon gone as they quickly dismounted and drew the pole aside for them to catch the solitary horse in the corral.

While Bert was transferring the saddle on to the new mount's back, his three companions entered the house and searched for food. A freshly baked loaf was quickly grabbed and also half a side of bacon which was hanging up.

'Come on, let's get outa here — pronto!' Tom Watts yelled.

They stepped over the bodies of the woman and the boy, who looked about ten years old. He was a nice-looking lad, thought Rory Yates. He had a brother of that age back home in Texas. It was then that a pang of remorse crossed his face.

'You didn't ought to have shot the woman and kid, Bert,' Yates said quietly.

'Are you against me now?' Bert demanded.

'No . . . but all the same . . . they didn't deserve to die.'

'Aw, shut up, Rory!' Bert spat. 'We've

left no witnesses. Come on, let's get outa here!'

But Bert Mayhew was wrong. There was a witness who had seen it all.

*   *   *

The posse were making steady progress in their search for the four wanted men. It was around five o'clock in the evening when they came to the homestead Bert Mayhew and his three friends had visited some hours earlier. The place was quiet, eerily quiet, Ray thought to himself as they rode towards the sod house.

As soon as they saw the three bodies the posse realized why.

'Do you reckon it was the four we're after who did this?' the lean, black-haired Bob Daniels enquired of the rest of the posse.

'I reckon so,' said Ray. He dismounted at the spot where the man lay, face down on the dusty ground. He turned the man over and they all noticed the bloody bullet hole in the man's heart.

They walked over to the woman and boy. Each had died from a single shot.

Ray entered the house, followed by the other three. Nothing looked disturbed but he guessed that the men had taken some food.

'We'd better bury them, hadn't we?' the ginger-haired Reg Toomy suggested.

Ray looked up at the grassy hill in front of them as they went outside again. Something caught his eye. He was sure he had seen a movement up there.

'Act natural,' Ray said. The others looked at him strangely. 'There's someone up there on the hill. Don't look up!' he warned urgently. 'I'm riding out and making a detour around so I come up behind them.'

'Don't you want us to come with you?' the blond-haired John Roday asked him.

Ray shook his head. 'No. Stay put and wait for me.'

It was impossible for the three to not to look up at the hilltop, but they did it carefully so the person or persons up there would not notice. Then they waited for Kinsella's return.

5

The girl tied the third rabbit she had shot that afternoon to the two others by a length of twine around its neck. The brown eyes had glazed over in death, but still appeared to be looking up at her reproachfully.

The rifle she had used so expertly was carried in her right hand and the rabbits in her left. She started back for home where she would help her mother skin and cook the rabbits. She had been taught to make pastry for the pie when the rabbits were cooked and was now equal to her mother in all cooking skills.

The sound of three shots came to her from the house. She stopped abruptly, her heart starting to beat faster. What was wrong? she wondered. Had her father shot at crows or other vermin? She had a sense of foreboding creep through her veins and she dropped on to her stomach and lay flat, peering over the grassy hill which overlooked the house.

There were four men below. They had just come out of the house, stepping over her mother and brother in the process. The prone body of her father lay several feet away from the door.

It seemed for a moment that her heart had stopped beating, then it raced both with fear and anger. She had to force herself to stay where she lay. To run down the hill and face them would only mean her own death, she was sure of it. She also realized that she might face worse at their hands before they finally killed her.

At last they left. She noticed that one of them was riding the family's horse and that a strange horse was left in its place in the corral.

She knew she would have to go down there now they had gone, but somehow she could not move. Her family were dead, but if she stayed where she was, she could pretend otherwise. She would put it off for as long as possible.

Tears fell down her cheeks, leaving grimy tracks. What was to become of her now? she wondered. She had no family and was miles from habitation. She realized she could not stay on in the house alone.

The hours passed. She had just decided that she would go down the hill and face the awful truth when she noticed four men riding towards the house. Were they the same ones? Had they come back for her? Had they seen her up on the hill before they left?

The girl raised her head slightly to get a better look at the men. No, she was sure these men were different ones. Perhaps she had better go down and talk to them, tell them what she had seen.

Something made her hesitate. What if these men were just as bad as the others? No, she decided she would wait, and watch.

The men went into the house and

came out again a moment or two later. One of them looked up at the hill and she ducked her head down quickly in case he saw her. They were talking together now, then a moment later she saw one of them, the one who had looked up at the hill, mount his horse and ride out the way they had come. She frowned. Why was he leaving the rest of the men behind? Where was he going?

★   ★   ★

Ray made his way around the hill and left his mount at the foot of it. He checked his gun before climbing up the grassy slope towards the man he was sure was at the top. He could see a form lying face downwards, but by the shape of it, he knew it was *not* a man. He came closer, slowly, silently, until he was close to her.

She turned with a small gasp of surprise. She made a grab for her rifle and Ray was upon her, grabbing at the gun and pushing the barrel upwards, away from him. Her finger was on the trigger and the sudden force caused her to pull it and the bullet whined harmlessly into the air.

It had been an instinctive reaction but Ray bunched his fist and hit the girl on the chin, knocking her out cold. She gave a small grunt as she fell back motionless.

Ray immediately regretted hitting her. It had been an instinctive reaction of self-preservation on his part. While she was unconscious he took the opportunity of studying her. She was a fine-looking young woman. He guessed her age to be about eighteen or twenty, hardly any more. She had thick, chestnut hair which came down to her waist. Her face looked grimy and on closer inspection Ray realized it was dried tearstains.

The pale-blue dress she was wearing looked shabby and old. In fact it looked as if she had grown out of it as it only came down to her calves. By the way the thin material clung to her body, revealing a shapely figure, Ray guessed it was probably the only dress the girl possessed. He moved towards her slowly. His hand came down on her body and he touched the material covering her breasts. Ray felt an unusual sensation run through him just then. He had never had a lot to do with women, neither had Fin. For one thing there were not many unattached females around and for another, women did not seem to want to make friends with either of them as they were so much alike it unnerved them. While she was still unconscious Ray ran his hands all the way down the girl's body and realized that the girl did not have any underclothes on beneath the dress. He drew his hand back away from her quickly. He had never felt like the way he was feeling right now, and it troubled him.

Seeing her there reminded him of a time during the war. The platoon Ray and Fin were in had come to a farm in

Kansas. There was only a young girl at home and about half a dozen of them dragged her into the barn and raped her in turn. Ray and Fin did not take part in the attack and Ray had never forgotten her screams. He had often wondered what had become of her. It seemed that women were seen as the spoils of war, at least as the war progressed, but Ray, for one wished this was not so.

Ray picked up the girl's rifle and also the three rabbits lying beside her. He was impressed with her skill at killing the three animals. It would soon be dark and Ray knew they would have to bivouac for the night and maybe eat rabbit stew for supper.

Besides the rifle and rabbits, Ray picked the barefooted girl up in his arms and walked down the hill to his waiting horse. He stowed the rifle and rabbits, lifted the girl up into the saddle and jumped up behind her.

As they came towards the house Ray noticed the men waiting for him nudge each other and mutter something.

'Damn me, if it isn't a woman!' Bob Daniels exclaimed. 'Kinsella ain't no better than the men we're trailing, shooting a woman!'

Ray overheard the last part.

'She's not dead,' he said. 'I was forced to knock her out or she'd have killed me. She's a pretty good shot too, if three rabbits are anything to go by.'

The three men grinned with relief.

'Did you *have* to knock her out cold?' John Roday asked him.

'Probably not,' Ray conceded, 'but I wanted to survive.'

He dismounted, propping the girl up while he did so, then pulled her from the saddle.

'I'll put her inside and cook these rabbits for supper.'

By the time Ray had skinned the rabbits, cut them up and put the pieces in the stewpot to boil on the range, the girl had regained consciousness. Ray was sitting outside at the time with the rest of the posse.

They glanced up as she came out. She walked straight up to Ray, looked him in the eyes and then gave him the biggest punch to his chin that he'd ever experienced, even from a man. He was shocked at how much it hurt. How could a slightly built young woman give such a punch? It would have been unbelievable if it hadn't happened to him.

The three other posse members were laughing out loud at what they had just seen.

She shook her hand at the pain from hitting him, then said,

'Now are you going to shoot me too?'

Ray rubbed his jaw ruefully. It really had hurt. 'Shooting you has never been my intention. Did you see the men who killed your family?'

She hung her head, tears not very far away.

'I didn't actually see them do it. I heard the shots and then saw them. One of them rode off on our horse and left his behind in the corral.'

'Was one of them wearing a blue shirt?' asked Ray.

She thought for a moment, then answered, 'Yes.'

'We're sure sorry about your folks, miss,' said the ginger-haired Reg Toomy. 'We'll bury them for you if you like? Where do you want them buried?'

The girl looked over towards a stunted oak-tree to the right of the house.

'Over there, in the shade. There are shovels in the barn.'

All four rose to their feet, fetched shovels and started digging three graves. When the last shovelful of earth was put on the third grave, the four stood back, their hats in their hands.

'Anyone know any words to say?' John Roday asked, looking at each in turn.

When no one volunteered, Ray began to recite the Twenty-third Psalm. As he did so, he realized that all of them, especially the girl, were watching him intently.

Ray finished the passage of scripture which he had delivered word perfect, and felt a little embarrassed.

'Fancy a bounty hunter knowing the scriptures!' exclaimed Reg Toomy in astonishment.

'I wasn't born a bounty hunter. I have done other things,' Ray informed him.

'How come you know those words so well?' the girl asked him with tears in her eyes.

Ray looked down at her beautiful face and felt he wanted to protect her, although she seemed pretty capable of taking care of herself.

'My twin brother and I were brought up by an aunt. She made us learn the scriptures by heart or we'd get a walloping,' he explained.

'What happens now?' the girl asked them all.

'We go in search of the men who killed your family — the same ones who killed my pa and brother,' said Ray.

'I'm coming with you,' she told them.

They looked at her incredulously.

'Oh no you ain't, miss,' Ray told her emphatically.

'Oh yes I am!' she stormed. 'I want to be there when you catch up with them, and I'm going to be. None of you will stop me.'

'What — dressed like that?' Ray grinned. 'You haven't even got any shoes on.'

The girl pursed her lips and placed her hands on her hips.

'I want no argument,' she said defiantly. 'I'm coming with you. I'll be ready in the morning.'

'That horse in the corral needs a shoe,' the blondhaired John Roday informed them. 'Unless we can fit a new one, you're going nowhere, lady.'

She thought for a moment, then said: 'Then you'd better fit one, or none of you is leaving here alive — and that's a promise!' She ran over to Ray's horse and pulled down her rifle. 'Understand?' she asked.

Ray ignored the question and walked

towards the house.

'I'd better check on that rabbit stew.'

'Do you understand me, mister?' she yelled after him.

'Yeah, yeah,' he replied without looking back at her, but waving an arm in the air.

The posse were all grinning at her behaviour and also at Kinsella's. They followed them both to the house.

The girl stopped the three men before they entered.

'Horseshoe first. Supper second,' she told them.

Bob Daniels grimaced.

'Aw, come on, boys. Let's see what we can do.'

The men, except for Ray Kinsella, walked off to the corral.

'Bossy, ain't she,' Reg Toomy grumbled.

6

An hour later three of the posse entered the house after shoeing the horse. The homesteader who had been shot a few hours earlier had obviously been loath to throw anything away and there were numerous horseshoes hanging up in the barn. Some were more worn than others, but Bob Daniels picked one or two of the best to match it with the three others already on the horse. Ideally they would have used a forge to heat and shape the shoe, but as there wasn't one, they had to make do without.

The girl produced metal plates for the men and was soon ladling out the stew that Kinsella had cooked.

They ate ravenously and their full stomachs made them feel drowsy and ready for bed.

'That was pretty good, Kinsella!'

John Roday congratulated him. 'Seems there's no end to your talents.'

The girl looked a trifle irritated at the praise heaped on the bounty hunter.

'You wouldn't have had it if I hadn't shot the rabbits in the first place,' she said through gritted teeth.

'We hadn't forgotten that, miss,' Ray answered. 'We can't keep calling you 'miss'. What's your name?'

'Kitty,' she answered.

'Kitty,' Ray repeated. 'Kitty cat.'

The others laughed, but the girl called Kitty did not even smile.

'We'll turn in for the night now,' Ray said for them all. 'We leave at sun-up in the morning. If you're coming with us, Kitty, be ready, suitably dressed for riding, or we go without you. OK?'

Kitty nodded. 'Don't worry, I'll be ready. You can all sleep in the barn tonight.'

Ray nodded and led the way through the doorway towards the barn.

★　★　★

The next morning at sun-up the men were saddling their horses. There was no sign of Kitty. In one way Ray was glad as he knew she would hold them up if she went along with them, but in another, he knew he would miss her, despite her antagonism towards him. He rubbed his chin and smiled. He could still feel it where she'd hit him.

Just as the men had mounted their horses, Kitty came hurrying out of the house. She was obviously wearing a pair of her father's trousers that came up to her armpits and held up by a belt. She also wore his jacket, hat and boots.

Ray let out a loud laugh at the sight of her.

'Dressed like that, girl, you'll frighten the criminals to death and we won't need to shoot them.' He laughed again.

They noticed her crestfallen expression at his cruel words and they all felt sorry for her.

'There's no need to say that, Kinsella!' the redheaded Reg Toomy told him indignantly. 'Whatever she's wearing, she still looks pretty to me.'

Kitty flashed Toomy a bright smile at the compliment. Why didn't Kinsella say something nice to her? she wondered. But she felt it was because he was still embarrassed by being hit by a girl.

She ran into the barn and dragged out a saddle for the horse she was to ride. It was Toomy again who came to her assistance, took it from her and saddled the animal.

Kitty looked at the man again with a dazzling smile on her face.

She mounted up and followed the men, hesitating for a few seconds in front of the three graves of her family. Her heart felt heavy with sadness, but she shook herself free of such feelings and urged the animal forward to start a new phase of her life. She had no idea if she would ever return to the homestead and in a strange way, she did not care either way. She knew she could not stay here alone. As she took another look back, she said a final goodbye to the place.

Kinsella kept to an even pace and appeared to know where he was going. By now the rest of the posse left it to him to lead them.

Kitty kept up with them without complaint and they all respected her. In truth, she was finding it hard going. She could ride, but had not done so often, and by mid-morning she felt she could not go on.

It was a great relief to her when the men stopped for a break. She helped fix a meal for them all and took a brief moment to lie flat on her stomach to ease the soreness she was feeling.

The men noticed the way she was lying and understood the pain she was in.

'You'd better let me rub some horse liniment into your rump,' said Ray. 'It'll get infected otherwise.'

'I'm not a horse, Kinsella!' she retorted.

'No, a mule more like! You're as stubborn and ornery as a mule.'

'Cut it out, you two!' Bob Daniels told them. 'You're acting like an old married couple.'

'Huh!' Kitty exclaimed. 'Kinsella, if you were the very last man on this earth, I wouldn't marry you!'

'Lady, if I was the very last man on this earth, there'd be no one to marry us!'

She thought about it for a moment or two, then added:

'If you *were* the last man left on earth, I'd go and live as far away from you as possible.'

To counter this, Ray came back with:

'Then you'd be responsible for ending the whole human race.'

'Good!' Kitty shouted. 'At least there wouldn't be any more like *you* left on earth!'

By now the other three men were laughing heartily at the entertainment put on for their benefit.

'Well,' Ray said, finding nothing more to add to her last statement, 'getting back to the subject of your rear end. If you don't let me apply some liniment to it and you can't ride any longer, we'll have to go on without you. You needn't think putting liniment on your rear end would give me any pleasure, 'cos it wouldn't!' he emphasized.

She thought it over for a second or two, realizing that they would indeed go on without her if she was unable to continue.

'Very well,' she conceded, 'just as long as it wouldn't give you any pleasure doing it.'

'Indeed it would *not!*' he emphasized.

'You others, don't look!' she ordered.

They grinned and turned their backs on the forthcoming proceedings.

Grudgingly, Kitty pulled down her pants to reveal a small, white bottom which was already becoming red. Ray rubbed some of the liniment into the sore skin very gently, but despite his gentleness, it still hurt — a lot. She gave an involuntary cry of pain, and the men with their backs to her, winced, almost feeling it for her themselves.

'There you are,' said Ray. 'That should help some. I'll put some more on tonight, then that should do the trick.'

She pulled up her pants and did the buckle of the belt up to secure them. She turned to look up at him.

'Thanks,' she said quietly. She noticed a tiny smile at the corner of his lips as he turned away from her and replaced the bottle of liniment in his saddlebags.

'OK,' said Kinsella. 'Time to ride again.'

The men noticed how she remounted her horse very gingerly and winced as she sat in the saddle.

'How far do you think we are away from the killers now?' Kitty asked Ray.

He made a quick calculation before answering her.

'There were about three hours between them arriving at your place and us turning up. Then another four hours before dark, so I reckon there's about seven hours' ride between us.'

'If it hadn't been for helping me, burying my folks, there wouldn't be so much ground between you and them,' said Kitty solemnly.

'True,' said Ray. 'But we couldn't have just ridden out and left you to do it yourself. I know you haven't a very high opinion of me, but I'm not *that* heartless.'

Kitty did not answer, but she was seeing a different side to Kinsella. Suddenly she felt cheeks crimson as she remembered how gently he had applied the horse liniment to her rear end. Maybe he wasn't as bad as she had first thought?

They rode in silence for the next few hours and it was around five in the afternoon when Kinsella called a halt. It was not before time, too. Kitty was feeling stiff and sore and she was uncertain as to whether or not she could dismount without falling over.

'Need any help, Kitty?' Reg Toomy asked her, coming round to her left.

'I think I might,' she answered, and looked quickly at Kinsella. She did not want him to know how bad she was feeling.

Reg assisted her to the ground and caught her when her legs began to buckle.

'I'm sorry I'm being a nuisance,' she told him quietly.

'You're no nuisance, Kitty,' he replied. 'Just ask me if you need any help.'

'Thank you, Reg.' She smiled up at him. 'You're very kind.'

A fire was quickly made and lit and the coffee pot produced. Kitty hadn't brought any food along with her as the loaf and bacon had already been taken by the men they were after. The three posse men were glad Kinsella had had the foresight to wake the man who owned the general store in Newton and bring provisions with them.

They cleared away and Kitty thought perhaps they would be spending the night where they were, but Kinsella had looked up at the sky and reckoned there were a couple more hours of light left before it became too dark to track the men.

Reluctantly Kitty remounted her horse, very slowly. Kinsella hadn't spoken to her since he had tended to her sore behind. He was a strange man, one it was very difficult to get to know well. All the same, there was something about him that fascinated her. Maybe it was his self-assuredness. He could look after himself and he did not seem to be a man who would be afraid of anything.

Darkness was almost upon them and Kinsella called a halt. After coffee and a few dry biscuits, Kitty cleared away.

Kinsella went to his saddle-bag and produced the liniment.

'Lie down and pull your pants down,' he told her. 'I'll put some more of this on you — and I *won't* enjoy doing it,' he added with a smile which she did not see.

'Well, that's all right then, Mr Kinsella!'

'My friends call me Ray,' he told her.

'I should imagine there aren't too many people who call you that!'

'You're right, miss. I'm careful who I call my friend.'

He turned from her and they all detected sadness on his face. Kitty wished she hadn't been so nasty, particularly as he had just tended to her rear end. But it was said. She would try and make amends in the morning, she decided.

7

Twenty miles away the four men whom the posse were trailing, Bert Mayhew, Rory Yates, Tom Watts and Nathan Ross, were settling down for the night by a creek at the edge of a small wood. The loaf and bacon they had stolen from the homestead was practically finished and the four knew they would need more food by tomorrow.

Rory Yates had been unusually quiet during their ride. He could not get the memory of the three Bert had killed at the homestead, particularly the boy, out of his mind. By riding with Bert and the others, it made him just as bad as them. He was no saint, he would readily admit to that, but at the same time he did have a conscience. If he told the others that he wanted to go on without them, how would they take it? he wondered. He shook his head. If he did

69

leave, then he knew he'd have to do it while the others slept, or they would not let him leave alive — Bert Mayhew wouldn't, anyway.

When it seemed that they were all asleep, Rory Yates crept out of his blankets and took them silently to the horses where he saddled his own.

'Going somewhere, Rory?' A voice came from behind him. He immediately recognized it as Bert Mayhew's.

'I . . . I thought it best if I went on ahead. I could find food and bring it back to you,' Rory stuttered.

'Oh yeah?' Mayhew asked scornfully. 'You're still upset about the killings at that homestead, aren't you?'

Rory did not answer and Bert continued.

'Don't fret yourself, Rory. I had to shoot them. They'd have told on us to the posse otherwise.'

'Told on *you*, Bert,' Rory reminded him. 'Me and the others didn't kill anyone.'

'We're all in this together, Rory, you

know that! Now come back to bed and forget about running off.'

Rory reluctantly unsaddled his mount and brought his blankets back to the fire. The others were awake and sitting up, watching what had happened.

'Rory here's decided to stay with us, boys!' Bert laughed. 'We must all stick together, ain't that right?'

'Yeah, Bert,' Nathan Ross answered for himself and Tom Watts.

'I don't reckon we can trust you any more, Rory,' said Bert. 'What are we gonna do about it, eh?'

'I won't run out on you again, Bert, honest!' Rory assured him.

'But how can I believe that? Have I got to stay awake all night and watch you? Well I can assure you, I sure as hell won't do that!'

'You *can* trust me, Bert,' Rory told him again, but his heartbeats were beginning to quicken. He knew he was now in danger.

'Sorry, Rory, but I can't trust you any

more.' Bert Mayhew pulled out his gun from the belt of his pants and fired at his former friend, at the same time saying, 'Goodbye, Rory. It was nice knowing you.'

Watts and Ross exchanged glances in the light from the moon. It was obvious that Bert Mayhew would treat them the same if they suggested they split up. They began to wish they hadn't brought him his horse so he could escape from Newton, that they had left him to face the consequences of his actions alone.

★ ★ ★

Kitty spent an uncomfortable night on the hard ground. It was not quite light and she needed to relieve herself. Now would be the most opportune time before the men awoke.

On her way back to the campsite she picked up dry wood for the fire until she had quite an armful.

As she stood up straight after picking

up the last stick she heard a footstep close by. It was Kinsella.

' 'Morning, Kitty,' he said. 'You're up bright and early. How are you feeling this morning?'

'Good morning, Ray. I'm very stiff if you must know. But I won't hold you all back, I promise.'

He noticed that she had called him Ray, it was the first time she had done so and it pleased him.

'Thanks for collecting wood,' he said.

'I must pay for my keep somehow,' she smiled a little. 'I'll go and put the coffee on. You'll want to make an early start, I reckon.'

'Yeah. We've got to make up for lost time. I'm not blaming you, though, Kitty,' he added hastily.

His tone was far less harsh this morning, Kitty noticed. Perhaps as from this moment they could be more polite to each other than they had been up to now.

'Ray, could we start over?' she asked, offering her hand.

Ray took it with a smile. 'Sure, Kitty. I'd like that fine.'

As Kitty arrived back at the dead fire, the men were now rousing and leaving their blankets one by one. She set to and soon had the fire alight and the coffee pot on to boil. She found the skillet, cut strips off the side of dried salt bacon and pushed them around with the point of the knife to prevent them burning. She put some sourdough biscuits on the metal plates. By the time the men returned to the camp the meal was practically ready.

'Come and get it, boys!' she called out to them.

They wasted no time, took the plates from her and ate ravenously.

Within fifteen minutes they were all ready to ride. Kitty put her left foot into the stirrup but she was so stiff she couldn't raise the strength to hoist herself up into the saddle. Reg Toomy was quick to notice. He jumped off his horse and pushed her rear end upwards.

She looked down at Reg, who, she guessed, was about Kinsella's age or possibly a little younger.

'I'm obliged to you, Reg,' she smiled.

'Any time, Kitty,' he smiled back.

They rode and Kitty knew Ray Kinsella would try and make up the miles between them and their quarry. However stiff she felt, she knew she must keep quiet and continue riding without complaint until Kinsella called a halt. This was at around midday. Another camp-fire was built and food and coffee produced, but this time Ray undertook the chores.

The stiffness Kitty had felt before was gradually beginning to disappear, for which she was very glad, and she no longer needed assistance mounting and dismounting her horse. She had spent so much time in the saddle that she felt she must smell like a horse by now, but she realized the others must be feeling the same. Oh for a good wash! she thought to herself as the rhythm of her horse's hoofs became ever more familiar.

The next day they came upon the spot where the men they were chasing had camped. They also came across the dead body of Rory Yates with a bullet in his heart.

Kitty gasped at seeing the man lying there. There had been no attempt at covering him.

'I wonder what happened for him to get shot?' She looked up at Ray and the others who had gathered around the body.

'He probably wanted to cut loose,' said Ray. 'Maybe he had become tired of riding with a killer.'

Kitty nodded, a dark frown on her face.

'What had seemed a good idea at the time, no longer seemed such a good idea,' Ray suggested.

'Do we bury him?' John Roday asked. 'I don't fancy bringing his body along with us. We don't know how long it'll be before we catch up with the rest of them.'

'I guess so,' Ray sighed. It would be wasting more time, but he felt he couldn't just leave the man where he was. 'He was some mother's son.' Two of them began to dig. It was a shallow grave, they only had small shovels with them. They all looked at Kinsella to see if he would utter any words over the mound.

'Lord, forgive this man his sins. Amen.'

'Amen,' the others chorused.

Seeing the dead body of Rory Yates and then burying him had affected Kitty more than she was prepared to admit, to herself or anyone else. It brought back memories of her family and how they had died. They were lying in their graves many miles away and she would never see them or speak to them again. She then realized how alone she was, in spite of being in the company of four men. When this was all over, what would happen to her? she wondered. She sighed and decided not to think about it any more. It would be no use wondering and fretting.

The ride continued.

8

Bert Mayhew and his two henchmen had arrived in Wichita. As yet, it was a normal town, but within another year it was to become a cowtown, plagued with all the trouble that went with that.

Their first visit was to the saloon, where they spent an hour slaking their thirst. They then made for a restaurant and ate their fill, pooling what little money they had left.

Their horses were thought of next and were given a good feed and water, and their hoofs were checked over. They did not think they were being followed as they hadn't seen any sign of a posse since they'd left Newton. They felt it safe to rest up for the night in a cheap boarding-house. They had dawdled since Bert had killed Rory Yates, sleeping during the day and only travelling for an hour at a time. That was their mistake and the reason that Ray, the posse and Kitty had made up for the lost time at Kitty's place.

It was around midday when the posse reached Wichita. They rode down the main street, looking about them as they went. There was no sign of the three men they were after. At Ray's signal they dismounted outside the saloon.

'Stay here, Kitty,' Ray told her. 'We'll go inside and take a look around. Maybe someone in there has seen them.'

'All right, Ray,' she said, and stood by the horses. She knew that if she had been a man she would have gone in with them, but she knew that women, except for saloon girls, did not go into saloons.

Kitty did not know how long she had stood there, but it seemed quite a while. No doubt they were all having a drink while she stood there like a fool!

She had just decided to enter through the batwing doors to see what was keeping them when three men rode down the street towards her. She watched them as there was nothing else for her to do just then. She didn't recognize them. They could even be the men they had been trailing for all she knew, as she had been too far away on top of the hill when they had visited her home to see their faces. Only Ray would be able to recognize the killer, who had been playing poker with him and his father and brother in Newton.

One of them looked hard at her as she stood there. She realized she must look a strange sight considering how she was dressed. The man even turned his head after he had passed her and looked at her again.

Kitty frowned. Surely she was not *that* interesting.

Then it hit her. She did not recognize the man, but she *did* recognize the horse he was riding. It was her family's horse, Toby. And he was not looking at her in particular, but the horse she had been riding — *his* horse!

Kitty's mouth opened in surprise.

She must find Ray. Immediately!

She stepped up on to the boardwalk and ran to the saloon. She pushed the batwing doors open and looked around her in the smoky room. Where was he, and the others?

A man was entering the saloon and tried to get past her as she was blocking his way.

'Mister, would you do me a big favour?' she asked him.

The bearded man in a black frock-coat looked bemused at her request.

'What can I do for you, miss?' he asked her.

'I'm travelling with three men — a posse after three men. One of them killed one of the posse's pa and brother, and this same man killed my pa, ma and brother. The posse went inside to ask around after them and I can't see them in there. The thing is, I've just seen the men we're after ride down the street just now. Could you ask for Mr Ray Kinsella and tell him that I've gone after the criminals before they get too far away?'

'But miss, you can't do *that*!' the bearded man exclaimed in alarm. 'Wait until you find your friends, the posse.'

'There's no time, mister! Please do this for me, right away! Don't let me down!'

Kitty hurried away and mounted her horse. She must not let the men get too far away. On the other hand, they must not see her.

The man with the beard and frock-coat went into the saloon and held up his hand.

'Anyone in here called Ray Kinsella?' he called out loudly.

Ray was at the bar with his back to the man and the other three were sitting at a table nearby.

'Who wants to know?' asked Ray, turning to face the speaker.

'A young woman asked me to tell you, the three men you're after rode past just now and she's gone after them. You'd better catch up with her pretty quick before she gets herself killed.'

A cold shiver ran down Ray's back at the man's words.

'Thanks, mister.' He patted the man on the arm.

'Come on, you three, Kitty's gone after the criminals on her own, the little fool!'

They shot up from their chairs and all rushed for the door. Ray was mounted first and did not wait for the others, who were soon behind him.

'If they know she's following them, they'll kill her for sure!' he yelled as he rode.

* * *

Kitty could see the men she was following in the distance. She sincerely hoped the man she had asked would find Ray and the others quickly. As she rode she began to realize just how stupid she was being. One of the men who rode her horse had obviously recognized his own and would now be alerted to the posse's close proximity.

She urged her mount forward. She must not let the men get out of her sight or they might double back and Ray could lose their tracks.

The men had entered a wood and Kitty began to feel afraid. Perhaps it would be better if she waited until Ray and the others arrived before she carried on any further.

She slowed her horse down to a trot then pulled it up to a complete standstill.

Suddenly, without warning, she was surrounded by the three men she had been trailing.

The man who was riding her horse took the reins of the horse she was riding.

'That's my horse you've got there, lady,' he said.

'And that's my horse you've got there, mister,' she replied.

He smiled slightly. She was brave, he gave her that. Any other woman would be screaming her head off by now, he reckoned.

'Where are the rest of them?' he asked her.

'Not far behind. You'd better give yourselves up before they kill you,' she suggested.

'They'd kill us if we did give ourselves up, so what's the difference?' Mayhew told her.

Kitty was thinking. What could she say to make them leave her and go on their way?

'Instead of hanging around, why don't you get out of here, now!' she suggested.

'Well now, we've got ourselves a bit of insurance. You can come along with us, lady, and then maybe your friends won't be too keen to shoot at us.'

Kitty couldn't think of an answer and allowed herself to be taken along with Mayhew holding her mount's reins. Her heart was beginning to beat faster with increasing fear. She felt sure she did not have long to live and the one thought that went through her head was that she would never see Ray again. Could it possibly be that she had fallen in love with the man?

$$\star \quad \star \quad \star$$

'Ray, we'll soon be crossing the border,' Bob Daniels informed him. 'We're all well out of our jurisdiction already. We've been out of the county for a long time now.'

'What you're trying to say is that this is as far as you intend going?' Ray prompted him.

'Well . . . yes,' Daniels answered slowly.

'OK, go back then,' Ray said tersely.

'Bob, we can't run out on him now!' said John Roday.

'I've never needed anyone before,' Ray told them. 'Go on, go back to Newton!'

'It won't be legal, but I'm staying with you, Ray,' Reg Toomy informed him. 'Kitty might be in danger right now. I'm gonna make sure she's safe before I quit.'

'Thanks, Reg,' Ray said, turning his head to look at the man.

'I'm staying, too,' Bob Daniels said. 'We can't leave you now, even though we're out of our jurisdiction.'

'Yeah, I'm in,' John Roday said.

Ray did not reply, but merely nodded. He was well aware that it was Kitty they all wanted to help. If she hadn't been with them they might have left him to get on with it on his own.

They rode for an hour and Ray guessed the three men and Kitty were riding hell for leather or they would have caught up with them by now. Ray was continually on the look-out in case they were bushwhacked.

He was becoming more worried. The longer Kitty was missing, the worse it would be for her. He was certain they must have her in their clutches by now. His blood ran cold.

9

Kitty was forced to hold on either to the pommel of the saddle or the horse's mane as Mayhew held the reins. They were galloping, hoping to put some ground between them and the posse.

'How many were with you, girl?' Mayhew asked her, glancing to his right as he spoke.

'Enough to bring you to justice!' she replied.

'How many?' he asked again.

'Four.'

'Huh!' he scoffed. 'One more than us. Only we're holding the trump card with you!'

'Don't bet on it, mister,' Kitty growled. 'If you hadn't killed one of your own men, the numbers would be even. Another thing, I mean nothing to the posse so you needn't think they'll hold back because of me.'

She noticed he gave her another glance and was obviously thinking things over.

'I wouldn't mind betting one or all of them have *some* feelings for you. You're not bad-looking under that hat.'

'Bert, we can't keep this pace up for long,' Nathan Ross put forward.

'I know that!' Mayhew answered scathingly. 'We'll make for them rocks up ahead and take cover. Pretty soon they'll come this way and we can bushwhack 'em. Then we'll have no more trouble.'

'More dead men to add to your list!' Kitty looked at him with contempt. 'Let's see, how many does it make so far? Two in the Newton saloon, three at the homestead, one of your own by the creek way back. By my reckoning, that makes six.'

They reached the rocks and dismounted behind them. Mayhew grabbed Kitty's wrist.

'Why were you riding with the posse?' Mayhew asked her when he'd forced her to sit on the ground.

'Because you'd wiped out my family and I wanted to see you all hang,' she told him. 'By the way, which one of you actually killed them? Or did you kill one each?'

'Tom and I didn't kill anyone, miss,' Nathan Ross told her. 'Bert here did all the killing.'

'I see,' said Kitty. 'But by riding with him and helping him escape from Newton, you're all just as bad in the sight of the law.'

Nathan Ross had been keeping an eye on the trail as she spoke and there was dust in the distance. Obviously riders were coming their way, and he reckoned it could only be the posse.

'We'll be having company shortly,' he said, pointing in the direction of the dust.

'Keep outa sight!' Mayhew ordered. 'They'll be like sittin' ducks.' He gave a short laugh.

Kitty's heart was beginning to pound at the thought of Ray and the men being killed without being given a chance of defending themselves. Whatever happened to her, she knew she'd have to warn the posse somehow and give them a chance to take cover.

'Here they come now!' Ross said.

'Wait for my signal, then fire!' Mayhew told them.

Kitty poked her head around the rock in front of her and saw that the men were within hailing distance.

'Look out, Ray!' she yelled at the top of her voice.

'Right, let them have it!' Mayhew ordered.

There was confusion for the first few seconds, but Ray motioned for the men to dismount and use their horses for cover. They had seen where the gunfire was coming from and when a figure emerged from the rocks, bullets were soon fired at them.

'Hold your fire if you know what's good for you!' Mayhew yelled from the rocks on the slight incline. 'We've got the girl and she gets it if you don't back off and throw your weapons down!'

'What'll we do, Kinsella?' Bob Daniels enquired.

Ray took only moments to consider Mayhew's proposal.

'If we throw down our weapons, we'll be shot anyway. *And* they'll kill Kitty as well, you can bet on it.'

Mayhew and his two men were all concentrating on the posse and it took only a moment or two for Kitty to take advantage of this. She crawled on her hands and knees towards her horse and pulled out her rifle from its scabbard, putting it quickly to her shoulder. She fired at Mayhew but he had already turned towards her, pulling the trigger of his revolver a fraction of a second before her whilst throwing himself to the ground, thereby evading Kitty's bullet.

A sharp pain shot through Kitty's left arm. It felt as though a swarm of angry bees had converged on the skin, all determined to sting her to death. She dropped the rifle, her right hand going straight to the pain. Her hand was covered with blood.

Kitty's actions had distracted Mayhew and his two men. Ray took the opportunity to rush towards the rocks, flattening himself against them. It appeared they had not seen him and he stayed in the same position, listening for any sign of their next move.

'Is she hit bad?' Nathan Ross enquired of Mayhew.

'Are you?' Mayhew asked her.

'What do *you* care?' she flung at him.

The blood was oozing through her fingers by now and she was beginning to feel a bit dizzy through the loss of it.

'You, down there, throw down your guns!' Mayhew yelled to the posse. 'The girl's been hit. Do as I say and I'll bind up her wound, otherwise . . . 'He left the sentence unfinished.

Ray was very worried now. He did not know how badly Kitty was wounded, but if he and the posse did give up their weapons he knew they would not be allowed to live. He knew he had to risk having a go now he was so close.

He eased himself around the protecting rock and took in the scene before him in an instant. All eyes were on Kitty, who was bleeding profusely.

Daniels, Roday and Toomy made a dash for the rocks as Ray had done a few moments previously. Ray was on the right so they moved to the left and inched their way around so that the three men were surrounded.

Ray was on his stomach. He looked to his left and saw that his three companions were in place, ready to strike. They waited for his signal.

'Get back to your places, boys. Keep your eyes open in case they make a rush for us!' said Mayhew.

The two turned away from Kitty and Mayhew. Ray took this opportunity to creep forward and force Mayhew's arm into the air, twisting it and relieving the man of his weapon. At the same time the posse came up behind the two cowboys and cracked their skulls with the butts of their guns.

'Tie their hands!' Ray shouted to the posse. 'I reckon I might have done this one a serious injury.' He quickly tied Mayhew's wrists together with the man's own bandanna and then attended to Kitty.

He tore the sleeve of her shirt off so he could inspect the wound. He was glad to see that the bullet had not gone through the bone, but nevertheless it had gone through the flesh and she was losing a lot of blood.

Ray used the torn-off sleeve to stanch the blood as best he could, then he tied his neckerchief around it.

'Will you be able to ride?' he asked her.

She nodded. 'What other choice do I have?'

Ray beckoned Reg Toomy over. 'Help Kitty on to her horse, Reg. The rest of us will have to get these killers back to Wichita. We might be able to put them in the jail for the night before we take them back to Newton.'

It took a while before the cowboys regained consciousness and they were helped to mount their horses, since their hands were tied behind their backs.

They moved off, back the way they had come. Ray knew they would not make it to Wichita before nightfall, and in a way he was glad that they would have to stop as Kitty needed to rest, having lost so much blood.

Kitty was grateful when Ray called a halt. He came around to her left and lifted her from the saddle. She swayed slightly and felt light-headed.

'Sit down while I unroll your blankets,' he told her. He looked at her arm, the makeshift bandage was saturated in blood.

'Anyone got something I can bandage Kitty's arm with?' he enquired of the men.

All three of the posse removed the neckerchiefs they were wearing and handed them over to Ray.

'I wish they were cleaner,' Reg Toomy said.

Ray nodded his thanks, untied his own neckerchief which he had used and removed the sleeve of her shirt which had been folded into a compress under it.

He took out the bottle of horse liniment from his saddle-bag and cleaned the bullet wound with some of it. Kitty let out a little cry at the pain it caused.

'Sorry about that, Kitty,' Ray said softly. 'It'll clean it a bit at least.'

She smiled up at him and allowed him to minister to her arm. It felt more comfortable, but the pain was almost unbearable.

Ray's blankets were laid beside hers. They were out of coffee beans and practically everything else. Ray had intended to stock up in Wichita, but they had been forced to leave before he had time to attend to it.

'You shouldn't have gone off on your own like that, Kitty,' he admonished her gently. 'You nearly got yourself killed.'

'I'm sorry, Ray.' She looked up at him as he leant over her on her bedroll. 'I couldn't see you inside the saloon and I couldn't let them get away.'

'How did you know they were the men we were after? You said you couldn't see their faces from that far away on the hill.'

'One of them kept looking at me, or at least I thought it was me he was looking at, but it was the horse I was holding. It turned out it was the one he left at our place when he took ours. I recognized the horse he was riding as our Toby.' She looked down for a second or two before continuing. 'I was a bit stupid going after them on my own, I know. I should have realized he'd connect me with the homestead where he killed my folks.'

'Maybe you were a bit stupid, but at least you warned us in time. We all thank you for that. We were riding into an ambush and could all have been killed if it hadn't been for you.'

'Ray,' she whispered so no one else could hear, 'I couldn't bear to let you all get killed, especially you.'

She looked up to see his gleaming white teeth in a smile.

'Try to get some sleep, Kitty. Wake me if you need anything in the night.'

'Thanks,' she answered, and snuggled down in her blankets. It felt comforting having him there beside her. The thought of him made her heart beat faster.

10

It was just a mouthful of water for breakfast, then they were soon all mounted up. It was only just light enough to see, but Ray was in a hurry to get back to Wichita and hand over the cowboys to the law, but most of all he wanted to find a doctor for Kitty.

Her arm did not appear to have bled much during the night and Ray decided to leave the makeshift bandages on the wound until they reached town. If they had ridden much further the night before, he knew Kitty might not have been able to survive the blood-loss. Rest was the best medicine for her.

The three tied-up cowboys were very quiet on their journey back to Wichita. They had all tried to pull their wrists free from the bandannas that tied them, but they had been unsuccessful. Luckily for the posse, the bandannas were made from strong material.

'You've gotta untie us,' Bert Mayhew whined. 'We need to have a call of nature.'

'Tough!' Ray spat. 'You'll just have to hold on until we get to Wichita.'

'But that's not fair!' Mayhew almost shouted.

'Life's not fair, mister,' Ray told him with menacing quietness. 'Killing my pa and brother wasn't fair. Shooting a man, woman and boy, wasn't fair. Even shooting one of the men who helped you escape wasn't fair. Now quit belly-aching or I'll shut you up myself. Permanently.'

★   ★   ★

The outline of the town came none to soon for everybody. They rode along the main street straight to the sheriff's office.

Ray alighted first and lifted Kitty down on to the boardwalk. He felt her stumble slightly and sat her down on a

101

plank seat outside the lawman's office.

'I'll drop these off and ask about a doctor, Kitty,' he told her. 'Sit there for a moment.'

She nodded and watched him and the posse escort the three cowboys inside.

The middle-aged sheriff stayed seated when they entered but looked interestedly at them.

'We're a bit out of our jurisdiction, Sheriff,' Bob Daniels explained, 'but Ray Kinsella here's a bounty hunter so he can go places where we can't.'

'What have they done?' Sheriff Patchett asked.

'He shot Kinsella's pa and brother in a poker-game in Newton. We followed them to a homestead where we found three bodies of a man, woman and young boy. The girl who lived there was up on a hill and kept her head down so they didn't see her. We came across her and she insisted on coming with us. Mayhew here, shot her in the arm yesterday. She needs a doctor.'

'Where is she now?' Patchett asked.

'I left her outside, Sheriff,' said Ray.

'Can you keep these men in your jail until we can take them back to Newton?' Daniels asked. 'With the girl being wounded, she won't be able to travel for a day or so.'

'The cells are empty at the moment, so I don't see why not,' Patchett said amiably.

He took some keys from a key hook by his desk and opened up the door leading to the cells. Daniels, Roday and Toomy escorted the cowboys to what was to be their new abode for a couple of days and untied their wrists, which by now had become blue through lack of a blood-supply.

'Where can I find a doctor for the girl?' Ray asked the sheriff.

'Turn right outside my office, down the alley and there's a house at the end. You can't miss it.'

'Thanks, Sheriff,' Ray nodded.

Patchett followed him outside as he wanted to take a look at the girl who

103

needed medical attention. He was surprised at the way she was dressed and a slight smile came to his lips. She looked in need of a bath and change of clothes besides having her arm attended to.

'Find us somewhere to stay for the night,' Ray said to Bob. 'Kitty'll need a room of her own and to have a bath laid on for her.' Ray handed over some dollar bills for himself and Kitty.

'The livery stable's to our left,' Patchett informed them. 'Down the first alley.'

They all nodded and Ray handed over the reins of his own horse and Kitty's to the men. They also led the cowboys' horses away.

Ray took Kitty's right arm, helped her along the main street and down the alley where the sheriff had directed him. He knocked on the door of the house which stood a distance away from the others. It was answered by a prim-looking woman with grey hair tied in a bun at the back.

'Is the doctor in, ma'am?' he asked her.

'Come in, young man. I can see who needs him,' she said with a slight smile as she looked at Kitty. 'John, there's a patient to see you!' she called into the rooms ahead of them.

A tall man with a grey beard and moustache came forward and beckoned Kitty and Ray into his surgery.

'Sit down, my dear,' he said kindly.

Kitty sat down gratefully as she was feeling rather shaky. She would have given anything for a cup of coffee right then.

'I'm Doctor Plummer, by the way,' he smiled down at her. 'What's your name?'

'Kitty,' she replied.

'And is this your husband?' Dr Plummer looked to his right at Ray.

Kitty smiled. 'No.'

As Kitty did not seem to want to inform him of anything else about herself or her companion, Plummer let it drop.

He carefully unwound the necker-chiefs which the posse had donated to help stop the blood and Kitty winced as some of the material had stuck to the wound.

'You've been shot!' he exclaimed.

'I know,' replied Kitty.

'Have you seen the sheriff?' he asked them both.

'We've just been there,' Ray explained. 'He told us where to find you.'

'Well at least the wound looks clean,' said Plummer, more to himself than anyone else.

'Ray here did some doctoring to it.' Kitty smiled up at Ray in thanks.

'I used some horse liniment. Would it have done any harm?' Ray asked.

'It's good stuff,' Plummer nodded. 'It has many uses, besides horses.'

Kitty gave a little laugh at this, remembering it being administered to her rear end a few days before. She did not enlighten the doctor about the secret joke.

Doctor Plummer was satisfied that there was no bullet lodged in Kitty's arm. He bathed and dried the wound, then applied some soothing ointment to it before bandaging it with a clean, white bandage.

'That should do for a day or two,' he said. 'Come back and see me then and I'll change the bandage.'

'Thank you, Doctor,' said Kitty.

Ray produced some dollar bills from the top pocket of his shirt.

'How much?' he asked.

'Two dollars,' was the reply.

Ray handed it over.

'I suggest you get as much rest as possible, young lady,' Plummer advised. 'And keep out of the way of men with guns. Nasty things, guns.'

'I couldn't agree with you more!' she said.

The doctor's wife ushered them out of the house and they returned along the alley to the main street, where they went in search of the only hotel in town. Ray hoped the men had managed to secure rooms for a couple of days, for Kitty would not be going anywhere for at least that long.

The posse were in the lobby of the hotel when Kitty and Ray arrived and the two walked up to them.

'Any luck with rooms?' Ray asked.

'Two doubles for us men and a single for Kitty,' Bob Daniels told him.

'Good,' said Ray. 'Did I give you enough money for our rooms?'

'I only booked for one night, so you've got some change coming.' Bob handed over the surplus money to Ray.

'The doc says Kitty should rest up for a couple of days then get her bandage changed. We'll pay for an extra night after tomorrow. Now let's see these rooms. I need a wash and shave.'

The others grinned. 'Like the rest of us!'

Ray helped Kitty to climb the stairs and Bob Daniels handed her a key to her room.

'They'll bring you a bath and hot

water in a few minutes, Kitty,' Bob informed her.

'Thank goodness!' Kitty sighed with relief at the thought of soaking away the smell of sweat, dust and a horse.

Ray quickly washed and shaved in his room which he was to share with Reg Toomy. Afterwards he left the room and hurried down the stairs and out into the street. Toomy assumed he was visiting Kitty as he had not explained his sudden exit.

Ray found a general store which sold clothes. He looked at the shirts and denims, picking out one shirt in a large size and two smaller ones. He also chose a pair of denims that were obviously not for him. Then he remembered something else. A pair of longjohns, small size.

He handed his purchases to the old man at the counter and took out some dollar bills.

'There are two different sizes here, sir,' said the storekeeper.'

'That's right,' said Ray. 'They're for

two different people.'

The storekeeper nodded and wrapped the parcels separately according to size.

Ray hurried back to the hotel and went up the stairs two at a time. He knocked gently on Kitty's door and immediately felt a little foolish holding a parcel of men's clothes for Kitty to wear.

'Who is it?' came Kitty's voice from the other side of the door.

'It's Ray.'

'Can you come back later? I'm in the bath right now.'

Ray thought it over but decided that Kitty would like to put the clothes on after her bath.

'I've got something for you!' he called.

'What?' she asked.

'Can you open the door?'

'Oh . . . just a minute,' Kitty said reluctantly. She had only just settled down into the beautiful hot water.

A few seconds later Ray heard the key turn in the lock and Kitty opened the door, a towel wrapped around her. She had washed her hair and it hung in wet strands over her shoulders.

'Can I come in?' he asked.

'Well . . . ' she hesitated.

'I won't take long,' he assured her.

Ray entered the room as Kitty moved aside. He shut the door behind him and faced her. His heartbeats quickened at her beauty and he suddenly felt tongue-tied.

Kitty smiled up at him, a questioning look in her eyes. He had obviously washed and shaved, which revealed how handsome he really was.

'I've bought you some new clothes,' he explained, handing over the parcel. 'You can change into them after your bath.'

'You're very kind, Ray. Thank you!' She took the parcel from him and put it on a chair. 'How did you know my size?' she frowned.

He shrugged his shoulders. 'I hope they're the right size. Well . . . ' he half-turned, then turned back to her and crushed her to him, kissing her firmly on her mouth which had been slightly opened invitingly.

'Ray . . . ' she breathed after he had released her slightly.

Then she found herself being lifted and carried over to the bed.

'Ray!' she cried out in alarm. 'What are you doing?'

She was laid on the bed and his body came on to hers.

'What I've wanted to do from the first moment I set eyes on you,' he declared, kissing her hard and long.

'But we're not married!' she broke in when his kisses ceased for a moment.

'That's hardly likely to happen, is it,' he scoffed. 'You told me I was the last man on earth that you would marry.'

The towel she had wrapped around herself had become unwrapped and Ray's long fingers began to investigate her body.

'No, damn you!' she screamed. 'What kind of a woman do you think I am? One of those saloon girls who give their body for the price of a drink! I know I owe you for a lot of things — the doctor, the room, the bath and the clothes. You know I've got no money to pay you, but I'm not going to let you rape me to pay for it all!'

He pulled away from her sharply at her impassioned words. He felt shocked. At his own behaviour as well as her outburst, which if he admitted it, she was well entitled to.

Ray stood up and pulled the towel back around her beautiful body. He could have kicked himself at that moment. He had ruined everything.

'I'd make a poor husband for you anyhow,' he said. 'I'd hardly ever be at home in my line of work. I'm real sorry for what I just did, Kitty. I don't like admitting it, but you're the only woman I've ever kissed. I guess you'll be the only woman I ever will kiss. I don't want anyone else but you.'

He strode to the door and opened it. Looking back at her tear-stained faced, he said:

'Please forgive me, Kitty. Goodbye.'

Kitty lay back on the pillow and felt unable to move. She realized then that Ray Kinsella was innocent where women were concerned. She had been the first woman he had ever kissed — or so he said. She gave a little smile. Ray Kinsella was the first man who had ever kissed her and she had acted like a child instead of a grown woman. He would never want to kiss her — or anything else — after this evening's performance.

Kitty sighed and walked over to the bath to resume her soak.

11

Kinsella leaned against the door of Kitty's room after shutting it behind him. He closed his eyes and ground his teeth together. What a mess he'd just made of it. Whatever must she be thinking of him right now? If only he could go back and start all over again. But it had happened and he could not undo it.

His eyes were still closed and the grinning face of his brother appeared to him.

'Why did you have to go and get yourself killed, Fin?' he said out loud as if speaking to him. 'I miss you like hell!'

It came to him then that if Fin had not died, he would never have met Kitty. Now that he had met her — and kissed her — and touched her — he would never get her out of his head.

Ray pushed himself forward from his

position against the door, clattered down the stairs and out into the street. The torches were being lit along the sidewalks and a piano was being pounded inside the saloon. He made his way there. A couple of drinks might make him forget the past few minutes, he reckoned.

He ordered a beer, took it to one of the tables nearby and sat down morosely, staring down at the brown liquid with the froth on top.

He did not see a saloon girl come up to him and her voice made him jump slightly as at first he thought it was Kitty. As if she would come to a place like this! The thought was absurd. How hurt she must have felt when she said he must think of her as a saloon girl.

'Want to buy me a drink, mister?' the woman asked, sitting down opposite him at the table.

'Not particularly,' Ray answered her, noticing the thick make-up she was wearing. He compared her to Kitty and how he had last seen her, her skin and hair fresh from her bath.

'You're not very sociable, mister,' the woman chided. 'Buy me a drink and I'll put a smile back on your face, I promise.'

'Get lost!' Ray growled.

She got up from her seat, her face as black as thunder.

'OK, suit yourself' she shrugged.

'I usually do!' he called after her.

Ray drank his beer slowly, considered buying another, then changed his mind. He'd get some sleep, he decided. Maybe things would look brighter in the morning.

★   ★   ★

It was around two in the morning when Ray awoke to the sound of pounding on his and Toomy's door.

'Kinsella, wake up! The prisoners have escaped!'

Ray was not fully awake. He wondered if he was coming out of a dream.

'What's going on?' Reg Toomy

grumbled sleepily.

'I don't know. I'd better find out,' said Ray, easing his longjohn-clad legs out of bed and standing up. He lit the lamp by his bed before crossing to the door and unlocking it.

'What did you say?' Ray asked the man standing outside.

'I'm the night marshal. The three men you brought in yesterday have escaped during the night. They killed a night policeman who was guarding them.'

'Hell!' Ray exclaimed. He turned back into the room. 'Reg, get your tail outa there! Did you hear what he said?'

'I sure did, Ray. We'd better wake Bob and John.'

Reg Toomy was pulling on his trousers while he was speaking, quickly followed by his shirt, then rushed from the room to the one next door.

'How long ago did this happen?' Ray asked the marshal.

'About an hour ago. I came back to the office after patrolling the town and found Wilf lying inside the cell with his head caved in. They've taken guns and ammunition.'

By now Bob Daniels and John Roday were fully clothed and leaving their room, their gunbelts on and carrying their rifles.

Ray dodged back inside the room, dressed hurriedly and checked his Colt before reholstering it.

'Will we need supplies?' John Roday asked Ray.

'No time. Make sure your canteens are full and let's go!'

'Hadn't we better tell Kitty?' Reg Toomy asked as they passed her door.

Ray thought for a second or two, then shook his head.

'Let the night porter know what's happening. He'll tell her in the morning.'

Reg frowned. He wondered if Ray and Kitty had been bickering again. It had appeared that they were getting on better yesterday, he thought to himself as he hurried after the others down the stairs. He quickly spoke to the night porter and made him promise to tell Kitty they would be gone for a while, chasing after the escaped prisoners.

The sheriff had been sent for and he was in the marshal's office when they arrived. To make things more legal he deputized Ray and his three companions, which would cover them up to the border.

They ran down an alley to the livery stables and fumbled for the matches to light the lamp so they could see what they were doing. Within five minutes they had saddled up and were riding out of town.

Ray guessed that they would still be heading for Texas, most probably following the Chisholm cattle trail. They were about fifty miles from the border and the Indian Territory of Oklahoma.

It was getting lighter and Ray made use of it to find the tracks of the three fugitives. The others looked to him and they were glad when he nodded and pointed ahead.

The posse made few stops during the next day and Ray was certain they were getting closer to their quarry. How would it all end? he wondered. A sudden feeling of foreboding crept over him just then. Would this be his final hunt? Was something telling him that he would not be coming back? He then felt Fin's presence beside him, but when he looked, he only saw Reg Toomy. How he wished Fin was riding with him again. He still felt as if half of him was missing.

★ ★ ★

The next morning they had been riding for an hour when Ray spotted a homestead in the distance. A warning ran through him. This was where it would all happen. He guessed Mayhew would use the occupiers of the log-built cabin as hostages to prevent them being fired at.

'Keep yourselves low in the saddle,

men!' Ray told them quietly. 'Try and approach the place under cover as much as you can. If possible, I want to arrive there without giving them any warning. We'll have more of a chance if we catch them by surprise.'

'Sure, Ray,' Bob Daniels answered for them all.

They approached slowly, quietly, and at Ray's hand-signal dismounted under the cover of a copse one hundred yards from the cabin.

Smoke was coming from the chimney but there was no movement from inside or near the place.

Ray used his hands to tell the men what he wanted them to do. He indicated that Bob should go round to the back of the cabin, John to the left side, Reg to the right and he himself would stay where he was, in front.

He put his finger to his lips for silence. He pointed to himself, held up his hand, then pointed to the cabin. They understood that he would give the signal for any shooting to begin.

It was a long wait — right up to midday and no one came out of the cabin. Surely they would have to come out soon. They must have animals to see to, Ray surmised. There were no horses in the corral, he noticed, or anywhere else for that matter. Were they wasting their time here? Had the fugitives moved off and were already crossing the border?

Ray felt he could wait no longer. He himself had access to water from his canteen slung on the pommel of his saddle, but the other three were nowhere near their supply.

Just then John Roday came up to him.

'Sorry, Ray, but I must have some water,' he explained his presence.

Ray nodded. 'I thought something would have happened by now. What the devil's going on in there?'

'Do you reckon one of us should go and take a look through the window?' John asked him.

'I'm beginning to think we better

had,' Ray answered quietly.

'I'll go if you like,' John offered. 'I'll go back the way I came and keep low. No one will see me from the side.'

'OK,' Ray nodded. 'I'll keep you covered from here.'

Ray watched as John Roday crept silently away and made his way to the side of the cabin. He looked over towards Ray for confirmation that no one had come out of the door. After Ray had nodded that all was clear, he hunched himself low and made his way to the window at the front of the cabin. Slowly, he inched his head and shoulders up until his eyes could see over the sill.

Ray watched Roday. He seemed to be taking a long time at that window. What was he seeing? he wondered.

Roday moved away from the window and stood up facing Ray. Ray saw him shaking his head, a bewildered expression on his face. He watched as Roday made his way back to him with the trees as cover.

'There's no sign of anyone in there!' John Roday exclaimed.

'Hell!' Ray growled. 'I reckon they lit the stove so it appeared that someone was at home, then left, probably taking the occupants with them.'

'Do you reckon?' John frowned.

'What other explanation could there be?' Ray shrugged his shoulders. 'We've wasted hours hanging around here and all the while they've been getting nearer to the border.'

'What if they cross it before we get to them?' asked John.

'You three will have to go back, but I'll go on. I'm getting them bastards, no matter how long it takes! And I'll do it with — or without you.'

12

Bob Daniels came around from the back of the house from the left and Reg Toomy came from the right. Ray and John Roday walked up to the cabin and Ray led the way to the door. He drew his gun just in case they had been fooled into thinking the place was empty.

Ray pushed the door open with his foot and stepped back a pace. It swung inwards on its leather hinges until it was fully open and Ray stepped forward, eyes alert and gun in a steady hand. He looked around the room as he stood in the doorway and was satisfied that no one was there.

The others followed him inside the place, which did not look as if it had been lived in for quite a while by the film of dust over everything. The stove had gone out.

'Any coffee around?' Reg Toomy asked hopefully.

'And food?' Bob Daniels enquired even more hopefully.

Ray opened the only cupboard and found some metal plates and mugs. There appeared to be no food at all in the room.

There was a coffee pot on the table which was cold and empty, three metal mugs, and plates which had obviously had a meal on them sometime that day, Ray guessed. He picked one up and sniffed it, wiping a finger over the slight traces of gravy.

'Smells like stew,' said Ray. 'The remains are still moist, so it can't be *that* long ago they left.'

'I reckon they must have left just before we arrived,' John Roday put forward.

'Yeah, I guess you're right, John,' Ray nodded. 'I must be slipping,' he admitted. 'I should have known they weren't here because there were no horses. It was the smoke from the chimney that fooled me. I just imagined them holding a family hostage as they've done a lot worse before now.'

'Don't blame yourself, Ray,' Reg told him. 'You haven't been wrong so far. They could easily have hidden the horses to make us believe no one was at home and then shot at us when we approached the house.'

Ray sighed and nodded his thanks to Reg for his support.

'There's no food here. They must have taken it all. The one and only time I didn't pack any and we can't get a morsel between us!' Ray punched his left palm with his right fist in annoyance at himself. 'I'm slipping up badly this time. I can't seem to think straight.'

Bob Daniels gave a small smile.

'Could it be that a certain little firebrand of a woman has messed with your head, Ray?'

Ray looked at Daniels in surprise, but he did not answer. Deep down, he knew the man was right.

'OK, let's get going! We're wasting time here,' Ray said, striding out of the door.

They mounted up once more, with only a sip of water from their canteens to sustain them. Reg Toomy looked about him for a rabbit or something edible as they rode.

It was around four in the afternoon when they left the cabin and the posse rode until seven o'clock. There would only be a couple or more hours left until nightfall. Ray was feeling more angry by every minute. The cowboys could not be so far ahead of them, he was sure of it, yet they had not come across them yet. He kept his eyes peeled for any movement up in the rocks to their right. He knew they would be sitting targets if the quarry were somewhere up there.

'Keep close to the rocks!' Ray told the three men by his side. 'If they *are* up there, they won't get such a good shot at us if we use the rock face for cover.'

The others nodded in agreement at the wise suggestion and moved their mounts in close.

As they rode, Ray found that his heart was beating faster. This was a sure signal to him that something was about to happen, and soon. The others noticed that he had pulled out his Henry fifteen-shot repeating rifle and they could feel the tension mounting.

Then it happened. Ray saw a movement up in the rocks ahead of them.

'Dismount and keep tight into the side of the rocks!' Ray ordered.

The three did not need telling more than once and they were ready for the flying bullets.

Ray's eyes were feeling blurred by the continual staring up at the rocks ahead of them. He blinked a couple of times so he could focus better. Then he saw the figure of a man walking towards them. He looked familiar. Ray watched him as he grew closer.

The three men with Ray were

alarmed at his next action and behaviour. He rushed out from cover and shouted:

'Fin! Keep down! Are you trying to get yourself killed?'

At the same moment he saw the movement again half-way up the rock formation. He let off a bullet from his Henry. A body came tumbling down, bumping on to rocks as it progressed until it hit the ground. His eyes saw another movement and he heard the sound of gunfire at the same time as he fired again himself. He had hit the rifleman and he too fell down the cliff face. There was silence then and Ray could not see another movement. Which two had he killed? he wondered. There was only one way to find out.

'Come on, Fin, let's get him!' Ray yelled as he ran towards the rocks ahead of them.

'Ray! Have you gone completely loco?' Bob Daniels shouted after the rapidly retreating Kinsella.

They followed him, keeping their

eyes up ahead, their rifles at the ready.

Ray reached the spot where the first body had fallen. It was one of Mayhew's friends. As he was looking at the dead man's face, a bullet whined past his right ear. Ray dodged back to one side and looked up towards the place from where the bullet had been fired. There was no sign of anyone.

A little further on Ray found the other body; again it was not Mayhew. That did it. He would climb up and get him. It crossed Ray's mind that the horses would not be able to get up there. They must be somewhere nearby, he guessed. If the posse captured the horses, Mayhew would not escape. If he would not come down from there, then they could leave him without a mount. Ray did not fancy his chances without one. A grim smile crossed his face at the thought. But he would rather catch the man and make sure of his fate.

Ray moved on, hugging the rock face for cover. Beyond the next boulder he came across three horses waiting patiently for their riders. He then saw a way up to the summit.

The posse had arrived by his side by now. Ray looked around him for Fin. A cold feeling ran down his back when it dawned on him that he had not really seen him, it had all been either a mirage or just his imagination. As he looked at the three men who were watching him anxiously, he began to feel rather foolish.

'I could have sworn I saw my brother, Fin,' Ray explained. 'You must think I've turned into some kind of crazy fool.'

Bob Daniels touched Ray on the arm.

'Being twins, you must have been much closer to each other than just two brothers. It's probably the grief still coming out, Ray.'

'Plus the fact you haven't eaten lately — like the rest of us.' Reg Toomy smiled, hoping to ease the situation. 'I'm beginning to think I'm seeing things that ain't there, myself!'

The others laughed and Ray felt a little less embarrassed at his behaviour.

There was now the next hurdle to get over.

'There's a route to the top here.' Ray pointed to the track.

'I'll come with you, Ray,' John Roday offered.

'OK, John. Keep your eyes skinned, you two. Guard the horses. We don't want Mayhew getting away.'

Reg and Bob nodded, and watched as Ray led the way up the track.

They needed to grip on to ledges and tufts of vegetation as they made their way up. It became awkward carrying a rifle and Ray wished he'd left it down below and relied on his revolver.

After about fifteen minutes they reached the top with a flat surface. Mayhew was waiting for them, a rifle in his hands.

'Drop your guns, you two!' the man ordered.

'Give me one good reason why we should do that,' Ray came back at him.

''Cos I said so. I've got you covered so don't try and be smart with me.'

'You're not being very smart, Mayhew,' Ray told him. 'There are two more of us down there,' he said, jerking his head behind him. 'Plus the horses. You won't get far without *them*. And another thing — there's only you left now your buddies are dead. *You* hand over your gun! You might get one of us, but the other'll get you.'

'I said, drop your guns. *Now!*'

While Mayhew was talking, Ray was looking over the man's shoulder.

'Are you cross-eyed or something? What are you looking at?' Mayhew demanded, wanting desperately to turn and see what it was that Ray could see behind him.

Ray could not see Fin this time, but he pretended that he could.

'Shoot him in the back, Fin! He don't deserve no other.'

The split second it took for Mayhew to turn his head slightly to face the man he knew he had already killed in

Newton was enough for Ray and John to open fire. Mayhew dropped forward on to his stomach, a look of amazement on his face. By Ray speaking to his dead brother, it had convinced Mayhew that Fin was really standing there, and this conviction had made the man see Fin, a smile on his face. In the second that Mayhew died, he knew Fin Kinsella had got his revenge.

13

The posse loaded the three dead men on to their horses and led them to the place where they had left their own mounts.

'Are we leaving these bodies in Wichita, or hauling them back to Newton?' asked John Roday of Ray.

Ray shrugged his shoulders. 'They're wanted in both towns since they killed the jailer in Wichita. Maybe they'll take them from us. It'll save a lot of trouble if they will.'

'We've saved both towns the cost of a court case and three hangings,' Reg Toomy reminded them. Reg turned to Ray. 'Will you be riding back to Newton, Ray — or go off bounty hunting again?'

Ray thought for a moment or two, then replied:

'I owe it to Fin and my pa to see that

they both have a proper funeral. Say a final goodbye. It won't be finished until I do that.'

Reg nodded understandingly.

'What about Kitty?' he asked him.

'I don't know, Reg,' Ray answered quietly. 'I really don't know what to do about Kitty. She's got to me more than anyone else has ever done. But I reckon I blew it with her. She'll find herself a man to take care of her, I dare say.'

'She'll have no trouble on that score,' Reg grinned. 'I might even ask her myself.' He looked searchingly at Ray to see what his reaction to this would be, but as usual, Ray's expression was inscrutable.

'Is there any food in the cowboys' saddle-bags?' asked Reg. 'Right now I could eat one of the horses.'

'Same here!' Bob and John echoed.

Bob felt in one of the saddle-bags and brought out some jerky. He cut off strips for each of them.

'This is all that's in this one,' he said.

John Roday tried another saddlebag

and found some stale, almost rock-hard bread. Reg Toomy could find nothing in the one he looked in.

'This'll just have to do — unless of course we find something to kill,' said Ray, and promptly started chewing on his slice of jerky.

Leading the horses made their journey back to Wichita a lot slower. It was not until they stopped for the night that Ray remembered that he had not left Kitty with any money. By now her arm should be redressed and she hadn't a dollar to her name, let alone two for the treatment. The sooner they got back to Wichita the better, he thought to himself as he lay down for the night and pulled the blanket over his head.

★   ★   ★

Ray and the others had been gone for two days now, and Kitty was bored out of her mind. She had been told to rest to make up for the loss of blood she had suffered through her wound, but the inactivity was sending her crazy.

She left her room and went down-stairs. The man at the reception desk called her over.

'Miss!'

She crossed the small lobby and walked up to the desk.

'Yes?' she asked.

'Will you be vacating your room today?'

Kitty frowned. 'No. I'll be staying until the posse gets back,' she informed him.

'The thing is,' the desk clerk began, a little embarrassed, 'no one has paid for your room. If you would like to pay now, you'll be able to keep it.'

Kitty's mouth opened in surprise.

'But I haven't any money,' she told him.

The clerk shrugged his shoulders. 'I'm sorry, miss, but my orders are to ask you to pay for the next week, or I'll have to let your room go.'

'But that's stupid!' Kitty exclaimed in mounting anger. 'Why should I pay for another week if I don't know how long I'll be staying? The posse will probably be back today, or tomorrow at most.'

The clerk shook his head. 'Sorry, miss, but I'll have to ask you to leave. May I have your key, please?'

'All right, if that's how you want it,' said Kitty. 'I'll just fetch my belongings and you can have your damn key!'

As she climbed the stairs again she was beginning to feel shaky with shock at being evicted from her room. What would happen to her now? she wondered. She gave a sigh when she entered the room. Oh well, she thought to herself, I've slept out in the open all the way from home, so it won't hurt me to do it again. I'll even sleep in the stables if I have to.

Kitty picked up her Spencer seven-shot repeating rifle and her father's jacket and hat. She left the shirt, minus the sleeves, and her father's trousers behind. She would let the hotel dispose of them. She was now dressed in the shirt and pants Ray had bought for her.

They fitted her well and accentuated her slim figure.

Satisfied there was nothing left behind that she wanted, she left the room and took the key to the reception desk.

'Here's your damn key!' she said, slamming it down. 'The sooner I get out of this rotten town, the better!'

Her anger had made her heart beat wildly and she stopped outside the hotel to recover slightly before walking off down the street. She knew she would have to find herself a job and get her arm attended to.

She passed the saloon where Ray and the others had gone when they had first come to Wichita to ask about the three men who had killed her family and Ray's. It did not enter her head to try in there for work. She made her round of the town, which did not take her long as it did not consist of many establishments.

The general store was her first port of call, but the owner and his wife were not in need of any help. She noticed how suspiciously they looked at her, dressed in man's clothes and carrying a rifle. She was to get the same reaction wherever she went.

The gunsmith greeted her with a smile when she walked into his shop. He was expecting this rifle-toting young woman to ask for a box of shells for her weapon, or even to buy a revolver perhaps? But his expression changed when she asked him if he needed an employee. Definitely not!

Kitty then walked down the alley to the livery stable. Perhaps they would let her clean out the stables, feed the horses, give them fresh water? No. No help needed.

'No one seems to have anything for me,' Kitty looked downcast when the livery stable-owner shook his head at her request for work. 'Can you think of anywhere else I might try?' she asked him. 'I've been to the general store, gunsmith, and you so far. There doesn't seem to be anyone else I can ask.'

'You're a pretty young woman,' he told her. 'Try the saloon. I'm sure they'll take you on there.'

'The saloon!' Kitty exclaimed in horror. 'Do I look like the type of woman who would work in a place like that?'

'Well . . . you seem pretty desperate,' was his reply. 'I didn't mean that you looked the type to work there though,' he said apologetically.

Kitty nodded. 'Thanks anyway. It doesn't look as if I've got any choice.'

The livery stable-owner watched her walk back down the alley. If she was taken on at the saloon, he hoped he'd see her in there tonight.

Kitty stood outside the saloon and breathed in and out slowly, trying to pluck up the courage to enter and make enquiries about work. She had no idea what kind of work it would be. Perhaps they'd let her serve the drinks, or sweep the floor?

She pushed open the batwing doors and walked up to the bar where the barman was polishing glasses.

He looked surprised to see her, especially dressed in man's attire.

'Yes, lady, what can I do for you?' he asked her, a mocking smile crossing his lips.

'Who's the boss man around here?' she asked him.

The barman inclined his head towards a man in the far corner playing pool by himself. He wore a white shirt, black vest and black trousers. He was tall, Kitty noticed and looked about forty years old.

'His name's Reuben Keech,' the barman informed her.

Kitty nodded her thanks and walked up to Keech. He eyed her briefly as he took a shot at one of the balls, which went as straight as a die into the far pocket.

'Yes?' he asked her with little interest in his voice.

'Mr Keech, I need a job. I was wondering if you could give me one?' Kitty asked hopefully.

Keech placed the end of the cue on the floor and held the tip in both hands, resting his chin on it as he looked her over. Kitty noticed the smile of amusement cross his craggy features.

'A job, you say? What can you do?' he asked.

'Well,' Kitty hesitated, 'I don't know. I've never worked for anyone before. I can cook. I can sew. I can clean the house. I can shoot rabbits.'

Reuben Keech threw back his head and laughed out loud.

'I can't say that I've ever seen any rabbits in here, so there's no call for a rabbit-shooter. I bet you've never even been with a man before, have you?' he grinned.

Kitty's mouth opened in surprise at the question.

'I should think not!' she exclaimed in horror. 'I'm not even married yet.'

'I thought so,' Reuben Keech nodded. 'I'm afraid you're a bit too innocent for a place like this, lady. You need to be as tough as buffalo hide, and you might hear words you've never ever heard before. The men who come in here aren't exactly churchgoers. Although there are one or two who profess to be good upstanding men of the community who come in here for some female company, if you see what I mean.'

Kitty looked him straight in the eye.

'Do you mean that the women who work here *have* to go with men as part of their employment?'

'They're not forced to,' he told her. 'Most of them like a bit of extra money though. I charge them for their room and food. I buy their clothes as well. In return they use their room for whatever purpose they want. Whatever they charge though, the house gets half.'

Kitty looked down at the floor and thought it all over.

'If they have to pay you for the use of their room, food and clothes, then I dare say they have to go with men to pay you back?'

He nodded. 'That's the deal. But as I

say, I don't force them to do anything they don't want to do, just so long as they pay me for what I've spent out on them.'

Kitty sat down on a nearby chair. She looked pale and upset, and Reuben Keech felt sorry for her.

'Why don't you find yourself a husband to take care of you, lady? You don't belong in a place like this.'

'Maybe not,' Kitty said, looking him in the eye again, 'but I don't have a cent to my name. I've been thrown out of the hotel because I can't pay the bill, I'm hungry, I need to go back to the doctor to get my arm fixed again. I'll just have to swallow my pride and do whatever you want me to do.'

Keech frowned. 'What's wrong with your arm?'

Kitty explained about her parents and brother being killed and how the posse who were after them from Newton came to her homestead and that she had insisted on riding with them and how she got shot by one of them before the posse brought them in. She told him how the killers broke out of jail in Wichita after killing the jailer and that the posse had left her in the hotel while they went off again in search of them.

'And the posse aren't back yet?' Keech asked her.

'No, and I'm left here without any money. If you employed me, perhaps you'd lend me two dollars so I can go back to the doctor to get the bandage changed?' Kitty asked hopefully. 'I'd also appreciate something to eat. You could take it off my wages.'

Keech looked thoughtful. 'If I handed over two dollars, what's to say that you wouldn't just walk out of here now and I don't see you again?'

'Here, take my Spencer,' said Kitty, handing over her rifle. 'It's a good one,' she assured him. 'When I've been fixed up with the doctor, I'll come back for it and . . . start work?' Her eyebrows raised at the question.

'OK. Here's two dollars. You can eat

when you get back,' he smiled.

Kitty left her jacket and the spare shirt wrapped up in brown paper that Ray had bought her on a chair. Another reason she would have to return to the saloon.

14

Reuben Keech watched the slim figure of the girl walk across the room and out through the batwing doors. A smile crossed his face. She had a good figure and he guessed she would look even better in a dress. Had he made a mistake in employing her? he wondered. She was hardly the type to work in his saloon, but he guessed men would find her attractive in a fresh, wholesome way, and would be glad to buy her drinks all night. She could even pay her way by doing this alone without having to resort to the thing she would abhor. It might not work out, but he would give her a trial. He was surprised how the girl had got to him as she was not his usual type. He could even feel something for her, given time, he thought to himself. She was so refreshingly naïve that it made him feel he wanted to protect her.

As Kitty walked down the street to the alley where the doctor lived, she began to have misgivings at what she was to undertake. Maybe everything would be all right and she might even enjoy getting men to buy her drinks. Then she had a sudden thought. If she had a drink from, say, a dozen men in a night, she would be rolling drunk! Oh dear, what had she let herself in for? she wondered.

The doctor's wife answered the door as on the previous occasion when Kitty knocked.

'Ah, you're back for your bandage change.' Doctor Plummer smiled. 'How has it been?' he asked as she removed her shirt, covering her breasts with it while the doctor cut the bandage away.

'It's hurt a bit, Doctor,' she told him. 'But it's a lot better now.'

Kitty winced when the doctor pulled the bandage away as it had stuck to the wound.

'Hm, it's healing up nicely. A couple

more days and it'll be as right as rain.'

'Good,' said Kitty. 'I'm starting a job today and I don't want any more trouble from it.'

'A job, eh?' he frowned. 'What kind of job?'

She hesitated. What would he think of her when she told him where she would be working?

'At the saloon,' she said. 'It's the last place I want to work, but I've got no choice. I've got no money for a room or food.'

'Really?' He sounded surprised. 'What about that young fellow who was with you last time I saw you?'

'He's gone off with the posse after criminals. I can't expect him to pay for everything. He's not related or anything. He's just one of the men I rode with after my family were killed back home.'

The doctor had been bathing the wound, then drying it while Kitty spoke. He finished by applying more ointment then rebandaging her arm.

'And do you think it's such a good idea — working in a saloon?' he asked her.

'Probably not,' she conceded, 'but I couldn't find work anywhere else in town, I tried everywhere.'

'I wish I could offer you work here, but there would be nothing for you to do. My wife helps me in many ways,' he explained.

'Never mind.' Kitty smiled. 'It will be a different experience for me at the saloon. I might even enjoy it,' she said hopefully as she put her shirt back on. She handed the doctor two dollars.

'Is it the same as before?' she asked.

He nodded. 'I thought you hadn't any money?'

'I borrowed it from Mr Keech at the saloon,' she explained.

The doctor saw Kitty to the door himself.

'Good luck to you, young woman. Goodbye. Call back if you have any more trouble with your arm, but I don't think you will.'

'Thank you, Doctor. Goodbye,' Kitty said, giving him a little wave at the other side of the door.

Doctor Plummer watched her walk the whole length of the alley and turn left for the saloon. He felt a little responsible for her, although he had no reason to be, he knew. He wondered if he would ever see her again.

Kitty walked through the batwing doors. Reuben Keech was still playing pool by himself. Didn't he ever get tired of it? Kitty wondered as she walked up to him.

'OK?' he asked her.

'Yes, it's almost better now. Is there anything for me to eat please?'

Keech beckoned the barman over.

'Bernie, get the young lady a meal. She'll be working here from now on — providing she fits in,' he added.

'Sure, boss. Come with me, miss and I'll fix you up with some food.'

Kitty smiled her thanks to both of them.

'When you've eaten, I'll get one of

the girls to find you a dress to wear,' said Keech.

After Kitty had eaten the pork and beans Bernie had provided for her, she was taken to one of the rooms upstairs and a tall, dark-haired woman came in with Reuben.

'So, this is the girl you've taken on, Reu,' she said with a sniff.

'She'll look better in a dress,' Reuben answered with a smile. 'Fix her up in something, will you, Clarice?'

'Sure, Reu.' She turned to Kitty. 'What's your favourite colour?'

'Blue,' said Kitty.

'Right, here's a nice red one here.' Clarice opened the wardrobe and brought out a red satin, low-cut dress with black chiffon roses round the neck.

'But I said blue!' Kitty reminded her.

'Red's more your colour. Blue's a bit pale for your skin. Men like girls in red anyway.' Clarice turned to Reuben.

'What's her name, Reu?'

'Kitty.'

'Kitty what?' asked Clarice.

156

'Kitty Brown,' came back the answer.

'I'll leave you to it,' said Reuben. 'Give her some tips on what to do, Clarice. See you tonight, Kitty.'

'Thank you for taking me on, Mr Keech.' Kitty smiled up at him.

'We'll see how well you do tonight. If you get more than a dozen drink orders, I'll keep you on, OK?'

Kitty nodded. 'Thanks again.'

* * *

The posse rode back to Wichita almost in silence. The constant reminder of the hours before were with them as they led the cowboys' horses with their late owners slung over the saddles. Ray hoped the Wichita law would accept the bodies and save them having to take them all the way back to Newton.

All four of the men were eager to get back into town again for something to eat and drink. Kitty was constantly on Ray's mind and Reg also thought of her possibly just as much. Reg wondered if

157

he dare approach Kitty, possibly ask her if he might call on her. But where would she be for him to call on? he wondered. He did not think she would be going back to her home. Would she go with Ray? he wondered. He would just have to wait and see what happened when they reached Wichita.

There were only a few more miles to go now. Ray suggested they keep going and not stop for the night and the other three agreed.

Ray was wondering how Kitty would greet him when he returned to the hotel. Would she ever want to set eyes on him again after what had happened in her room? He kicked his mount in the flanks to quicken the pace. He had to see her.

★   ★   ★

It was six in the evening and Kitty started her evening's work. There would be more customers as the evening progressed but Kitty was glad there were not too many in yet so she could get used to the job gradually.

There were four girls altogether working for Reuben Keech, including Kitty. At first two of them seemed a bit hostile towards her and Kitty was at a loss to understand why as she had never met them before. It hadn't occurred to her that as she was much prettier than them, they were afraid she would get more customers.

Clarice had taken Kitty under her wing on Reuben's instructions and when Kitty had asked her how she could stay sober after so many drinks bought for her by the customers, Clarice laughed.

'Don't worry, Kitty. They're mostly water with a bit of colour to them. The customers don't know that though, even though they pay for the real thing.'

Kitty frowned. 'But that's cheating!'

'Oh, Kitty!' Clarice rolled her eyes in despair at her innocence. 'You've got a lot to learn, girl! Now circulate and *smile*!'

Kitty left her teacher and walked around the tables smiling. She did not feel she could keep it up all evening or her face would ache.

'Come and join us!' a young fellow of around twenty said, pulling Kitty down on to one of the chairs beside him. Three other young bucks were grinning broadly.

'What's your name, miss?' the same young man asked her.

'Kitty,' she replied.

'Kitty what?' he asked.

'Kitty Brown.'

'Well, Kitty Brown, can we buy you a drink?' he asked, his blue eyes twinkling.

'Thank you very much,' said Kitty and gave him a big smile.

The young man got up and walked to the bar. Bernie had been watching and knew he'd have to provide a watered-down version without the customer noticing.

While he was gone, the three other men at the table started to make

160

conversation with Kitty.

'You're new here, aren't you?' a fair-haired one asked her.

'My first night. I've never been in a saloon before.'

The three frowned. They hardly believed her.

The first young man returned with her drink and Kitty drank it down quite quickly. All four sat with their mouths wide open.

After Kitty had drunk the special brew, she stood up.

'Well, gentlemen, it was nice talking to you. I must circulate. I'll perhaps see you again.'

'Oh come on!' they urged. 'Stay a bit longer. We'll buy you another drink.'

Kitty shook her head and smiled. 'Sorry, but it's the rule of the house not to stay with a customer for too long. Others might get jealous,' she added, and eased herself away from the table in search of other customers. The evening had just begun.

15

It was around midnight when Ray and the posse arrived back in Wichita. They called in at the sheriff's office and delivered their charges.

'What happens now?' Ray asked. 'Have we got to haul the bodies all the way back to Newton, or as they killed a deputy, will Wichita take care of them?'

'I guess it will be OK to leave them with us,' said the night policeman. 'Did you have a shoot-out, or did you sneak up on them?'

'They were above us in the rocks. We shot two of them and went up after the third — Mayhew, the real killer — and we got him.'

The policeman nodded. 'OK. You'd better sign this paper and that'll be it as far as you're concerned.'

Ray nodded. 'Thanks. We're glad it's over with.'

He and the posse members decided that it wouldn't be worth looking for a bed for the night, as most of the night was over.

'I suppose I'd better check on Kitty.' Ray looked from one to the other. 'I don't suppose she'd be too happy if I woke her up though,' he added. 'Let's get a drink.'

'We're with you there, Ray!' Reg Toomy smiled.

After unloading the bodies and carrying them into the back of the sheriff's office, they all walked along to the saloon. It was always Ray's custom to stand inside the door and survey the room before moving to the bar and ordering a drink. As the hour was late, the room was more smoky than earlier and the place was full. He noticed four saloon girls walking among the tables, stopping now and then when they were offered a drink. He was glad Kitty was not one of them.

Ray ordered for the four of them and they each carried a beer to one of the unoccupied tables and sat down. They all felt tired — and hungry. Maybe the place served food as well.

One of the saloon girls moved up to them. Ray did not take much notice but he glanced up. Then his mouth dropped open.

'Kitty?'

The other three men grinned.

'Hello, Kitty. What're *you* doing here?' Bob Daniels asked for all of them.

Kitty looked directly at Ray. 'This is where you think I belong, isn't it, Ray?'

He turned and grabbed her wrist. 'Of course it's not! Why are you here?' he demanded.

Kitty pulled her wrist away. 'I had no choice, Ray. I was thrown out of the hotel because the bill hadn't been paid, and every other place in this town didn't want my services so I had to come here.'

'Come on, you're getting out of here,' Ray told her, standing up and grabbing at her wrist again.

'No I'm not!' she retorted. 'I can't let you pay for everything for me. I've got to stand on my own two feet from now on.'

He took her by her shoulders and looked down into her velvety brown eyes. He desperately wanted to kiss her, but here was not the place.

Someone came up behind her just then, it was Reuben Keech.

'Stop bothering the lady, mister!' he told Ray.

'I'm not bothering her. She's my fiancée,' Ray declared.

Kitty gasped in surprise.

'No I'm not! He's never even asked me to marry him!'

'Come on, Kitty, let's go!' Ray urged.

Kitty's very first customer of the evening had been drinking steadily with his friends and he did not like the way Ray was pulling at her.

'Leave Kitty alone!' he shouted, stumbling forward drunkenly, his gun already in his hand.

Ray half-turned, but not fully. 'Keep

165

out of this, mister. It's between me and my fiancée.'

'You haven't asked me to marry you. You haven't even said you love me!' Kitty flung at him.

Before Ray could answer, there was an explosion close by and Ray felt the impact of a bullet like a mighty thump as it entered his left shoulder. He gave a short gasp and felt himself falling to the floor, almost knocking Kitty over in the process.

'Ray! Oh no! Ray!' Kitty yelled, kneeling down beside him as the blood oozed from his back.

'Someone — fetch Doctor Plummer!' Kitty screamed. 'Hurry! Give me something to help stop the blood!' She looked around her as she spoke.

Bernie the barman hurried forward with some glass-drying cloths.

'Will these be enough, Kitty?'

She folded them and pressed them into the oozing wound, but the blood did not seem to stop gushing.

'Has someone gone for Doctor

Plummer?' she called out, almost in tears.

'Yes,' Keech answered. 'Someone, get hold of that drunk!' he ordered as the young man who had shot Ray stood there swaying, his gun held pointed at the floor.

The young man's friends came forward, relieved him of his pistol and dragged him out of the saloon before he did any more damage. They all thought it would be a good idea to get out of town — quick.

After what seemed an eternity to Kitty, Doctor Plummer came hurrying in, carrying his bag.

'Move out of the way!' he ordered, and the onlookers moved back so he could come through. He did not need to ask what had happened and knelt down beside Ray, pulling away the towels from the bullet wound. He tore Ray's shirt so he could get a better look at it.

As Ray was lying face down, the doctor could not see if the bullet had gone straight through or whether it was still lodged inside.

'Hold those towels hard against his wound while we turn him over a bit. I need to see whether the bullet's still inside him.'

Bob Daniels helped turn Ray slightly and the doctor took a quick look. He shook his head.

Plummer looked up at Keech. 'Is there a room we could put him in?' he asked.

Keech was not too happy about it. It was bad for business.

'He can go in my room, can't he, Mr Keech?' Kitty implored.

Keech thought for a moment then nodded.

'OK. But I'm not paying any doctor's bills for him.'

'Ray's got some money,' Kitty told him. 'Thanks, Mr Keech.'

Bob, John and Reg helped to carry Ray upstairs to Kitty's room. When he was settled on the bed Kitty scurried away to fetch hot water and more towels.

It took quite a while before Doctor Plummer was able to take out the bullet, clean up the wound and bandage it. He looked up at Kitty's worried face as she stood beside him, handing him instruments and towels to mop up the blood.

'You and your man seem to be taking it in turns to get shot,' he remarked, a smile crossing his lips.

'It looks that way,' said Kitty. 'Is he going to be all right, Doctor Plummer?'

'Like you, he lost a lot of blood. As long as infection doesn't take hold, he should be all right within a few days. He won't be able to do any shooting for a while. It'll feel very stiff.'

'Will you call on him again?' Kitty asked worriedly.

'I'll come and see him tomorrow some time. Get word to me if he's any worse before then.'

'Thanks a lot, Doctor. I'll have to look in Ray's pockets for some money to pay you.'

Plummer shook his head. 'He can

pay me himself when he's fit. He won't be going far for a while. I can wait.'

Kitty smiled her gratitude and escorted Plummer to the door. Bob, John and Reg were still in the room and they could tell how worried Kitty was about Ray.

'Will the owner of this place let you stay with him?' Reg asked her.

'I don't know, Reg,' she shook her head. 'I should think the place will be closing soon anyway. I think I should keep working here for at least until Ray's ready to ride again. It'll help pay for my keep and the doctor's bill.'

'We'll call around tomorrow, Kitty,' John told her. He took another look at Ray who was still out cold. 'Do you think you two will be getting married when he's well enough?'

Kitty smiled slightly. 'If he still remembers he's asked me, then yes, I think we will.' She ushered the three men out of her room. 'Goodnight, boys — or should I say, good morning?'

' 'Bye, Kitty!'

170

Kitty sat in the chair by the bed and watched Ray as he slept. She thought of what had happened in her hotel room before he left with the others during that night. It had been a new experience for her — and also for him. Maybe together, after they were married, they could try again and she would show him that she really did love him.

16

When Ray opened his eyes the next morning, it was only just light. His shoulder hurt a great deal and he was not in the same bed he'd had at the hotel. Where on earth was he?

Someone was in the chair by his bed. A woman wearing a red satin dress with some black material around the low-cut neck. What was she doing there? She looked as if she was asleep, her head had dropped forward so he could not see her face clearly.

He waited. When it got a little lighter he might get a better look at her.

What on earth had happened to him the night before? Was he in some saloon-girl's bedroom? If so, what had happened between him and her? He couldn't remember anything. He did remember, however, his clumsy attempt at making love to Kitty in her hotel room. Where was she now? he wondered.

An hour later, after drifting in and out of sleep, the room was lighter and when Ray opened his eyes again, he saw that the woman by his side was Kitty! What was going on? Why was she dressed so gaudily with rouge on her cheeks and lips? Ray gasped at the transformation from the fresh-faced woman who had met him at the door of her room with just a towel around her after getting out of the bath.

Kitty made a mumbling sound as she raised her head on wakening. Her neck ached through sleeping in the chair all night. She looked quickly at the bed and saw that Ray was watching her.

'Ray!' she exclaimed, a beaming smile on her face. 'How do you feel?'

She stood up and bent down to look at him closer. He was very pale.

'What am I doing here, and what are *you* doing here — dressed like that?' he asked, frowning deeply.

'Don't you remember?' she smiled. 'I

173

work here. You came in and . . . ' She hesitated. Should she remind him that he had told everyone present in the saloon that she was his fiancée? No, she would let him remember this for himself. She did not want him to feel he was being forced to keep his word. Maybe this morning he would have changed his mind?

'Someone shot you in the shoulder and the doc had to get the bullet out. You'll be laid up for a while,' she informed him.

'Who shot me?' he asked. 'Was it Mayhew?'

'No,' she smiled. 'I didn't ask last night as there was so much going on with you being shot. But I think you must've brought him and his two cowboy friends in. I don't know if they were dead or alive. A drunk customer shot you. He didn't like seeing you try to drag me out of the saloon.'

Ray was quiet for a few minutes, thinking over everything Kitty had told him, then it all began to come clear in his mind.

'I can't remember why you're working in a place like this,' he said.

'I needed the money, Ray. When you left with the other three, I had nothing — not even a hotel room when they made me leave.'

'I should have left you some — I'm sorry, Kitty. You don't have to work here any more now that I've come back.'

'I can't let you pay for everything, Ray.' She shook her head. 'I need to be able to take care of myself. You won't be around all the time.'

Ray was frowning again, trying to remember something from last night.

'Kitty . . . Did I ask you to marry me last night?'

Kitty smiled and shook her head.

'Not exactly,' she said. 'You did inform everyone in the saloon that I was your fiancée, though.'

'Oh.' He looked down at the sheets. 'Did you say you would — marry me, I mean?'

'No, because you didn't ask me.'

'Well I'm asking you now — not that I'm much of a catch,' he added.

'I might do,' she said mysteriously. 'But only if you tell me one important thing.'

'What's that?' he frowned.

'Ray, if you don't know what it is, then I can't marry you!' she exclaimed. 'I'll get you some coffee and breakfast.' And with that, she left the room, her head held high.

Ray lay there in Kitty's bed and tried to think. What did she mean? What was it he had to tell her before she'd marry him? He shook his head and waited for Kitty's return.

About fifteen minutes later Kitty entered the bedroom carrying a tray of coffee, egg and bacon, together with two slices of rye bread.

'I hope you feel up to eating this,' she said, placing the tray across his legs in the bed.

She could see that he looked far from well and knew the pain must be quite

176

bad. His wound was even worse than hers had been and hers had hurt a lot.

'I am hungry,' he told her. 'Me and the boys hadn't eaten for a whole day and night when we got back. I hope they found somewhere to eat.'

Kitty sat by the bed while he ate, but she could see beads of perspiration on his forehead and she knew he was in a lot of pain.

'The doctor should call in some time. Maybe he'll give you something for the pain,' she said.

'I could sure do with something,' he nodded.

He ate some of the food, but could not finish it. He drank most of the coffee though.

'You'd better give the owner of this place some money, or he'll throw me out.' Ray tried to smile, and looked around him.

'Where's my shirt?' he asked her.

'I took it to wash. If you're looking for your money, I put it in here for safe keeping.' Kitty opened the drawer of a closet and handed him the roll of banknotes. Another folded piece of paper was with it.

'What's this?' she asked, handing it to him.

'A wanted notice on someone. Open it up for me, will you?'

Kitty opened the sheet from its squares and held it up for Ray to see.

'You won't be catching up with him yet awhile,' she told him.

'I haven't looked at it for some time. I almost forgot what the fella looked like,' said Ray after memorizing the black bearded face.

''Black Jack Thompson'.' Kitty read out the name of the wanted man. 'He's an evil-looking varmint. I bet if he shaved off his beard, you wouldn't recognize him even if you bumped into him.'

'You might be right at that!' Ray smiled.

The perspiration was dripping off him by now and Kitty took the tray from him and poured some water into a bowl.

'I'll give you a wash, Ray,' she said. 'You're burning up!'

The cool water felt marvellous to Ray and he felt a little better for a while, but very soon he became delirious. Kitty was very worried by now.

There came a knock on the door. Reg Toomy stood on the other side.

'How is he, Kitty?' he asked when she opened the door to him.

'Reg, I'm worried. He's burning up and started babbling. The doctor said he'd call round sometime, but I think he ought to come now.'

Reg Toomy took a look at Ray and knew Kitty was right.

'I'll get him, Kitty.'

Kitty watched him run down the stairs and through the saloon to the outside door. She hoped Doctor Plummer would arrive soon.

Ray had pushed the bedclothes away from him and was moaning quietly. Kitty bathed his forehead again and his chest, which was covered in dark hairs.

'Don't you dare die on me, Ray Kinsella!' she admonished. 'You've got a wedding to go to!'

She tried to get him to drink some cold water, but he was thrashing around too much for her to be able to put the glass to his lips.

It seemed a long time before Doctor Plummer and Reg Toomy arrived. The doctor took one look at Ray and Kitty could see the man was worried about him.

'I've been bathing him with cold water, Doctor,' Kitty told him.

'Good girl!' he said. 'We've got to get his temperature down and that was the best thing you could have done.'

He took a small piece of folded paper and asked for a glass of water. Kitty handed it to him and the doctor poured the white powder from the paper into it.

'Now I want you to put your arms around his shoulders and hold him steady while I try to get him to drink this. It'll help with the pain.'

Kitty sat on the bed beside Ray and did as she was instructed. Between them they managed to get Ray to drink some of the mixture.

'Give him the rest in a couple of hours. I'll come and see him again this afternoon.'

He looked at Kitty and she could see concern for her on his face.

'You ought to get some sleep, young woman, especially if you're working here again tonight.'

Kitty nodded and smiled. 'I'll try to get a few minutes if Ray settles.'

'Yes, do that!' he ordered. 'You won't be much use to him if you don't get any rest yourself. Right. I'll see you later on today.'

Kitty thanked him and he left. Reg Toomy stayed in the room.

'Can I do anything for you, Kitty?' he asked with concern.

She shook her head. 'Thanks, Reg, but no. When are you and the others going back to Newton?'

'We had planned on going today, but we'd like to stick around a bit to see how Ray goes.'

Kitty nodded. 'Thanks for dropping by. Come again when you want.'

Reg Toomy walked down the stairs of the saloon and out into the street. The sun was shining and the town was beginning to come alive. He walked back to the hotel and joined his two friends. He knew they were all eager to get back home and hoped it would not be too long before Ray recovered enough to ride. He thought about Kitty. It seemed as though she and Ray had got together, in spite of all their bickering on their way to Wichita. Reg Toomy smiled to himself. He'd had a feeling it would happen.

17

While Ray was sleeping after Doctor Plummer's painkilling powder had relaxed him, Kitty took off her dress and hung it up in the closet. She put on the denims and shirt she had worn previously and lay beside Ray on top of the bed. She hoped she would be able to catch a few minutes' sleep before he woke up again. As her head touched the pillow she realized just how tired she was and hoped she would not be disturbed for a while.

When she awoke a couple of hours later she turned and looked at Ray. His eyes were open and he was looking at her. He smiled.

'Ray!' she exclaimed. 'How do you feel now?'

'My shoulder hurts like hell!' he said, his voice coming out cracked and dry.

She hurried round to the other side

of the bed and picked up the glass with the rest of the mixture in it.

'You're to finish this up,' she told him. 'It might ease the pain some.'

She supported his head while he drank it down, grimacing slightly as he swallowed the powder at the bottom of the glass.

Kitty bathed his forehead and face again and was glad that his fever was not quite as bad as before.

Ray settled back on the pillow and when Kitty was sure he was asleep again, she lay down beside him and managed to get another hour or so herself.

At around noon Kitty went downstairs to the kitchen, to prepare herself some food and get something for Ray. Reuben Keech came into the room.

'How is he?' he asked.

'A little better, I think,' she said with a smile.

'You didn't tell me you'd got a man when you asked for a job.'

'I hadn't,' said Kitty. 'Not really

anyway. Nothing was ever said to make me think anything would happen between us. Most of the time we argued and sniped at each other.'

Reuben smiled. 'I have the feeling Kinsella's a man of few words and can't exactly express what he really feels.'

Kitty turned from the table where she was cutting herself some bread.

'I think maybe you're right, Mr Keech.'

'Reuben,' he corrected. 'Are you still working for me, Kitty?'

She nodded. 'Yes, I'd like to. I'm not married to the man yet and I want to keep my independence until, or if, we marry.' She hesitated for a moment and looked him straight in the eye. 'Mr — er, Reuben — will you allow me to check on Ray now and then during the evening?'

Reuben sighed. 'I guess so. Just so long as you don't spend too much time with him. Understand?'

Kitty nodded. 'Thanks.' She gave him a big smile.

'If you're getting Kinsella something to eat, make sure it's easy on his stomach. He won't fancy a big meal and it wouldn't do him any good lying there like that. That's the advice my granny always gave anyhow!' Reuben added with a laugh.

'Then I'll take your granny's advice, Reuben.'

Reuben Keech watched as she left the room. Pity she'd got herself a man, he thought. He quite fancied her for himself.

★   ★   ★

After a few more visits from Doctor Plummer, Ray seemed to have improved and was now sitting up in the chair beside the bed. He missed Kitty when she was working and was glad when she called in to see him now and then.

When Bob, John and Reg were satisfied that Ray was on the mend, they decided that it was time to leave for Newton. They were well overdue back and guessed there would be speculation on their long absence. They called in to see Ray and Kitty for the last time.

'We'd better get going now, Ray,' Bob Daniels told him. 'Everyone back in Newton will think we're all dead.'

Ray nodded. 'I understand. Thanks for everything, boys. When I'm ready to ride, I'll look you up in Newton.'

'Just you?' Reg asked him, looking at Kitty as he did so.

'Maybe the two of us will look you up,' he smiled.

They left Kitty's room with a wave as they reached the door. Both Kitty and Ray knew they would miss them. They'd become close over the past weeks.

★   ★   ★

Two weeks passed and Ray declared himself fit to leave. Kitty was not sure if she was glad or not, for it meant giving

187

up her job in the saloon. She had quite enjoyed it while it lasted, but it was not something she would have liked to do for any length of time.

Ray paid his dues to Keech, and Keech paid Kitty what he owed her — more than she was expecting. Keech had been well pleased with the money she had brought into the place with her winning smile.

Ray's arm was still in a sling, but Doctor Plummer gave him the all clear to ride, providing he took constant rests.

Kitty bade farewell to the friends she had made and left her room with Ray. She was dressed in the denims and shirt she wore on her first day there, and carried her trusty Spencer.

At the top of the stairs Ray stopped and looked down at the saloon. It was around ten in the morning and not too many men were down there. Kitty gave him a quick look and then surveyed the room herself. There was a certain man at the bar who looked vaguely familiar to her. Where had she seen him before? Then it came to her. Black Jack Thompson. The man on Ray's poster.

Had Ray recognized him? she wondered. Her heartbeats began to quicken. If he had, what would he do? Would there be more gunfire, and would Ray get killed? He only had the use of one arm at the moment. If he had recognized Thompson, surely he would not try to arrest him while he was recovering from a bullet wound?

Ray started down the stairs without saying a word. Maybe he had forgotten about the poster? Kitty thought to herself hopefully. Should she mention about Thompson or just walk out into the street without saying anything? But Ray had already asked her to help him buckle on his gun belt before he'd left her room, so he was obviously making sure he would be prepared for any gun play should it occur.

Ray took Kitty's arm and propelled her through the saloon and out of the batwing doors into the street. Kitty sighed with relief that he had not noticed Black Jack Thompson. They could leave town without any trouble.

'Kitty, here's some money. Fetch our horses from the livery. I've got something to attend to.'

Kitty's mouth opened in astonishment. He *had* seen Black Jack, and he was getting her out of the way while he attended to the business he did for a living.

'No, Ray!' she implored. 'Don't go back in there! *Please* don't do it! You're not fully fit.'

He gave a short laugh. 'I've worked when I've been worse than this, Kitty. Now do as I say and bring the horses back here!'

'Ray, there's still something you haven't said to me.'

He flashed her a look, his brow furrowing.

'What's that?' he asked her.

'I told you before. If you don't know what it is, then we don't get married.'

She looked up at him defiantly, slight anger showing in her voice.

'What do you want me to say?' He looked down into those beautiful eyes of hers. 'That I love you?'

'Yes!' she almost screamed. 'You've never — ever — said it to me.'

He smiled. 'I'd hardly be marrying you if I didn't love you, now would I?' he demanded.

'You still haven't *said* it, Ray Kinsella. Do you love me?'

'Kitty . . . I've never known the meaning of the word. Except for Fin, I've never loved anyone before in my whole life. The feeling's new to me, Kitty. I've only just found out what the word really means. I *do* love you. Yes, I really do.' He kissed her very briefly on the lips and turned to go back into the saloon.

Kitty's heart seemed to fall, and she suddenly felt an icy tingle creep through her body. Was this how being with Ray would be like all their life together — her wondering if she would ever see him again each time he left her to go on his man hunts? She didn't think she could take it. It would be like having her heart torn out each time he left.

18

Should she do as Ray told her and fetch the horses, or should she wait outside until he came out? She knew he would not want her to go back inside as he would be distracted by her presence when he did what he knew he had to do. It was his job and he had done it for many years now. But he had always had back-up before — Fin, and then the posse. And another thing: Ray's left arm was in a sling and he was still weak from his injury.

Despite what he had told her, Kitty decided she would wait outside. They could collect the horses together, later, when he had arrested Black Jack.

Kitty walked up to the batwing doors and was just able to look over them into the room inside. Black Jack was leaning on the bar, facing the doors. He needed to see who entered and left the saloon.

Ray walked past the man without looking at him. Kitty frowned. It was as if he hadn't seen him standing there. She noticed that he went up to the bar and stood behind Black Jack. He obviously ordered a drink as Bernie produced a bottle and a glass. The outlaw had not paid him much attention. A man with an arm in a sling could hardly do him any harm.

The next thing happened very quickly and Kitty almost missed it. Ray pulled out his revolver and pressed it into Black Jack's back. She couldn't hear what was said.

'Take your gun out real slow, Black Jack, and put it on the bar, barrel facing you!'

Ray pushed his own weapon harder into the man's back as an added inducement.

Black Jack began to draw his gun out of its holster slowly, but just as he had put it down on the bar, the explosion of a bullet being fired behind Ray rang out. Black Jack had not been alone. He had a friend who had shot Ray in the back.

Kitty felt a scream in her throat but no sound came out. Ray fell to the floor.

Black Jack came running out, quickly followed by the man who had just shot Ray. Kitty moved to one side to let them pass. She realized she still held her Spencer and without thinking, put it to her shoulder, drew a bead on Black Jack and fired. Without waiting to see the man fall, she did the same again, bringing down the other outlaw.

A crowd soon gathered around the two bodies and everyone looked in amazement at Kitty, her Spencer still in her hands.

She quickly pushed the batwing doors open and ran up to Ray. From where the bullet was positioned in his back, she knew without touching him that he was dead.

Bernie leapt over the bar and came to her and Reuben Keech hurried forward.

Reuben expected Kitty to be crying beside Ray's body by now, but she stood motionless, looking down at his back. She felt Reuben's arms around her shoulders and the feeling of his warm hands helped a little to thaw her seemingly frozen body.

Reuben felt her begin to tremble and knew that shock was setting in.

'Get her a whiskey, Bernie!'

Bernie soon brought one over to her where she sat at one of the tables beside Reuben, who held both her hands in his.

Kitty took a sip of the whiskey and shuddered at the taste.

'Drink it down, but slowly!' he warned. 'It's the real stuff, not one of the 'specials' you usually drink.'

When the last of the drink was finished, Reuben looked up as Sheriff Patchett strode in and came straight to Kitty. He glanced briefly at Ray's body on the floor.

'Who shot him?' he asked Reuben.

'A stranger. Ray there' — he pointed

to him — 'was arresting a man at the bar. Another man shot Ray in the back and they both ran outside.'

'And I gather that you, young lady, shot both of the men who were running away?'

Reuben's mouth opened in surprise.

'Is that right, Kitty?' he asked her, a smile crossing his face.

She merely nodded.

'Ray Kinsella was a bounty hunter,' Reuben explained. 'He obviously recognized the bearded one and if it hadn't been for his partner shooting Ray in the back, Ray would have brought him in.'

Reuben looked again at Kitty. 'I figure you should get the bounty on him — or *them* if they were both wanted men.'

'The bearded one's name is Black Jack Thompson. The other one is Linus Marx. Between them they're worth one thousand dollars. If you'd like to call in at my office, I'll give it to you, young lady. What's your name, by the way?'

Kitty did not answer. Tears had begun to fall.

'Her name's Kitty Brown,' Reuben told the lawman. 'I'll bring her along when she's not so upset. She had just left my employment and was going to marry Ray Kinsella, so you'll understand how she's feeling at the moment.'

The sheriff nodded.

'Sure. I'm sorry, miss,' he apologized. 'When you're feeling up to it.'

Kitty ignored him. Bounty money was the last thing she could think of at the moment. She moved from the chair and knelt down beside Ray and put her arms around his shoulders.

'Help me turn him over,' she looked up at Reuben.

The saloon owner did as she requested and turned Ray over on to his back so Kitty could see his face.

'Why did you come back in here, Ray?' she demanded of the lifeless body. 'Why couldn't you have left this one and gone back to Newton with me as you said you would? Well, at least you won't have to marry me now, will you? You knew it wasn't such a good idea, didn't you? It would never have worked out, you and me, and you knew it.'

Reuben could see her shoulders shaking but the tears flowed silently.

⋆　⋆　⋆

Some time later Wichita's undertaker called to collect Ray's body.

'Who's the next of kin or friend?' he asked, looking round at Reuben, Kitty and Bernie.

'I was his fiancée,' Kitty said brokenly. 'I'm taking his body to Newton for burial next to his brother and pa. I'd like a horse and buckboard waiting for me in the morning with Ray's body on board.'

'Kitty, you can't take him all that way on your own!' Reuben exclaimed in amazement.

'I'll manage,' she said. 'I've got to cope on my own from now on, so I might as well start tomorrow morning.'

Kitty looked up into Reuben's grey eyes. 'You've been good to me over the past few weeks, Reuben. I appreciate all you've done for me and Ray, letting us stay here.' He opened his mouth to answer but Kitty broke in. 'If you'd do just one more thing for me?'

Reuben nodded.

'I'd like to stay in my room until tomorrow and make an early start for Newton.'

'Of course. But do you have to go there? I'd like you to stay. In fact I'd like you to stay here for good. I'd take care of you, Kitty,' he told her earnestly.

'No, Reuben,' she shook her head. 'Ray wanted to go back to Newton to say goodbye to his brother and pa, so it's what I must do for him — it's the last thing I can do for him.'

Reuben took her hands in his. 'You could always come back afterwards,' he told her. 'I'll be waiting.'

Kitty smiled. 'I can't think about anything just now, Reuben. I'll see when I reach Newton.'

'Come on, I'll escort you to the sheriff for the bounty money. I'm sure Ray would want you to have it. You'll need a bit of money of your own now.'

Kitty thought about it for a second or two, then nodded.

'Yes, I think he would want that.'

Reuben took her arm and walked her down the street to Sheriff Patchett's office.

A strange feeling crept over Kitty when Patchett handed her the thousand dollars taken from the safe — the money that should have been Ray's.

'That was pretty quick thinking on your part, miss,' said Patchett. 'They could have got away and it would have meant forming a posse and all the trouble that entails.'

'I know all about posses, Sheriff,' said Kitty. 'I rode with one to Wichita.'

19

It would take Kitty between two and three days to reach Newton, she reckoned. She called in at the undertaker at 8.30 the following morning and the buckboard on which was Ray's coffin, together with a fine-looking horse were waiting for her.

She paid the man and placed her Spencer at the side of the seat before jumping aboard. She had said her final goodbyes at the saloon but she would have to pass it on her way out of town.

Reuben, Bernie and Clarice were standing outside the batwing doors and they waved and said goodbye as she passed.

'She ought to have someone with her, Reu,' Clarice remarked when Kitty was nearly out of sight.

'I reckon she'll manage,' he smiled. 'She can use a rifle — and not just for rabbits!' He laughed as he remembered the day she had asked him for a job, one of her qualifications being that she could shoot rabbits.

★　★　★

At around midday on the third day, Kitty could see the outskirts of Newton ahead. She smiled to herself at the way she had handled the buckboard and fixed food and coffee along the way. She had depended on Ray and the others to reach Wichita, but she felt quite proud of the fact that she had not needed anyone on the return journey.

The red-headed Reg Toomy was also driving a buckboard along the road out of Newton. He could see a figure in the distance which seemed vaguely familiar, but he did not recognize Kitty until he was almost on top of her. They recognized each other at the same moment.

'Kitty!' Reg yelled.

'Reg!' she yelled back.

They stopped their buckboards side by side, each of them equally glad to see the other.

'Where's Ray?' Reg asked her, a frown on his face.

Kitty inclined her head behind her and Reg noticed the coffin on board, covered by a tarpaulin,

'But . . . but I thought he was almost fit again when we left!' he exclaimed in alarm. 'Did he have a relapse or something?'

Kitty shook her head and Reg was quick to notice a tear come into her eyes.

'He'd picked up a Wanted poster in Newton when he delivered the body of another criminal. We were leaving Wichita to come back here together when he spotted this man in the saloon. He took me outside then went back in.' Kitty hung her head, finding the words difficult to speak.

'He'd disarmed the man, but a friend of his in the saloon shot Ray in the back,' she explained.

Reg jumped down from his buckboard and came up to her.

'Oh Kitty . . . I'm so sorry!'

'I've brought Ray back for burial next to his brother Fin and his pa,' Kitty explained. 'He so wanted to be able to say goodbye to them before he decided what we were going to do.'

'Fin.' Reg sighed.

Kitty frowned at the way he said the name.

'When we were after Mayhew and his two friends — when we left you behind in Wichita — Ray kept seeing his brother and talking to him. It sure scared the hell out of the rest of us!' He shook his head at remembering it.

Kitty lowered her eyes and Reg thought he detected a tear in them.

'I don't think Ray would ever get over losing Fin, Reg. I feel certain I would never match up to him — ever. Fin would always come first in his thoughts and me a close second. If I had married Ray, I would have married Fin as well.'

Reg nodded. 'I know what you mean, Kitty. So you and Ray didn't get married before he was killed?'

Kitty shook her head. 'It would never have worked out. I knew that when he went back into the saloon in Wichita to arrest Black Jack Thompson. It was somehow as if it had to happen the way it did. I won't ever forget him, but I know now that if Ray had lived, I wouldn't have married him. I couldn't have taken all the partings each time he left on a job.'

'Kitty . . . ' Reg hesitated, looking at her closely. 'I don't know if you ever knew, but I fell in love with you on our way to Wichita.'

She did not answer him, but gave him one of her special smiles.

'Where are you going, Reg?' she asked.

'To the lumber yard about a mile out of town.'

'Are you doing some building or something?'

'All kinds of things,' he grinned.

'From coffins to buildings and everything made of wood in between. I've
got my own business in town. I do
pretty well,' he told her, hoping Kitty
would be impressed.

'You're not married then — or got a
woman?' she asked.

He shook his head and grinned
again. 'I'd like it fine if you'd take me
on, Kitty.'

She smiled. 'I'll surely think about it,
Reg. I'll call in at the undertaker's now
and I'll see you in town later. I'd like
you to be by my side when I bury Ray.'

'Kitty, I'd be happy to be by your
side for ever!' he declared.

She beamed him another smile,
flicked the reins of the horse and it
started off again.

As she rode the buckboard down the
main street she noticed a man dismounting outside the town marshal's
office. He had been leading another
horse with a body tied over its back.
Kitty felt a stab to her heart. It was as if
she was witnessing Ray at the end of

one of his jobs. The man looked in need of a shave and his clothes were trail-worn and dusty. Their eyes met as he stepped up to the boardwalk but he showed no interest in her.

Kitty carried on down the street and pulled the horse to a stop outside the undertaker's and went inside.

She made the arrangements for Ray's funeral with the special request where he was to be laid to rest. It would take place the next day.

'Are you the next of kin of the deceased?' the undertaker asked her.

'More or less,' she said. 'We were to be married.'

'Both Mr Kinsellas had money on them when they were brought in here,' the undertaker told her. 'As you're so close to them and I don't know of anyone else to give it to, you'd better have it. I've deducted the cost of the two funerals from it. There's quite a tidy sum,' he said, producing some dollar bills from a metal box in the corner of the room.

Kitty's mouth opened in surprise. What with the money given to her for killing Black Jack and Linus Marx in Wichita, she was now comfortably off. She accepted it and put it in the pocket of her denim trousers.

'If a Mr Toomy comes asking where I am, will you tell him I'm at the boarding-house.' Kitty had seen it before she went into the undertaker's.

★   ★   ★

The next morning Reg called for Kitty at the boarding-house. She wore a new dress of dark blue and a hat of the same colour with a wide brim, which she had bought in Newton the previous day. It was the first time he had seen her in a dress since the first time they had met at her homestead.

'You look real fine, Kitty,' he told her.

'Thank you, Reg. You look pretty good yourself,' she smiled, noting his black suit and black string bow tie.

She took his arm and they followed

the preacher and Ray's horse-drawn funeral carriage to the graveyard on a hill. The grave had already been dug next to his brother and father.

As Ray's coffin was lowered into the ground, Reg put his arm around her shoulders. He felt her body shaking and knew she was crying.

'They are all reunited now,' Kitty breathed. 'I'm sure this is what Ray would have wanted.'

Reg nodded.

Kitty took Reg's arm as they walked back down the hill. It felt very natural to Kitty and she felt at ease with Reg. She looked up into his blue eyes as they walked together. He was honest, kind and uncomplicated, and she was very glad he was with her just then.

Reg did not ask her to marry him again. Today was too soon. Time was what Kitty needed right now. But Reg intended being there when the right time came.

BLIND TRAIL

Mark Bannerman

Whilst on military patrol for the United States Cavalry, Lieutenant Raoul Webster is blinded in a freak accident. Guided by his young brother, he sets out for San Francisco to consult an eye doctor. But, en route, their stagecoach is ambushed by ruthless Mexican bandits. Raoul's brother is murdered, as are the driver and all the male passengers. Raoul survives, but he is alone in the wilderness and vulnerable to all Fate can throw at him. He is kept alive by one burning ambition, to track down his brother's killer . . .

SIX-SHOOTER JUNCTION

David Bingley

Deputy Sheriff Sam Regan considered he had been lucky when he found an outlaw's horseshoe mark outside the Bankers Hotel in Blackwood after a bank raid. He overtook a raider and was badly shaken to learn that the outlaw was Pete Arnott, a boyhood friend. The meeting, however, led to gun play and Sam had to kill Pete. He tried to hide the fact that Pete was an outlaw, but the truth leaked out to certain important people who insisted on Sam chasing the raiders and proving the link between Pete and the gang . . .

FLINT'S BOUNTY

Ben Coady

The town of Eagle Junction has two headaches — the prolonged drought and the threat of revenge from the Galt gang. Having killed Ben Galt, brother of the notorious Jack Galt, the marshal has fled town. His deputy, every bit as alert to the danger, has followed his example. Meanwhile, Dan Straker, a drought-stricken farmer, is loading up his last supplies from Arthur Flint's store. Without supplies he's done for and Flint can no longer extend credit to him. Then, a dangerous option is revealed to Straker . . .

LOBO AND HAWK

Jake Douglas

One was a Yankee. One was a Rebel.
They were the only two survivors of
the bombardment of a New Mexico
town at the end of the Civil War.
After trying unsuccessfully to kill
each other, they decided to become
partners and go after some Confederate gold that was up for grabs.
The trouble was that they weren't
the only ones who knew about the
hoard. Soon there would be trouble
enough to bring back old hostilites,
and only blazing guns would settle
the matter. But who would live?

HONDO COUNTY GUNDOWN

Chad Hammer

The Valley of the Wolf was no place for strangers, but Chet Beautel was not the usual breed of drifter. He was a straight-shooting man of the mountains searching for something better than what lay behind. Instead, he encountered a new brand of terror enshrouded in a mystery which held a thousand people hostage — until he saddled up to challenge it with a mountain man's grit and courage, backed up by a blazing .45. If Wolf Valley was ever to be peaceful again, Chet Beautel would be that peacemaker.